Truly, Madly Megan

Stella Etc.

Karen McCombie

Truly, Madly Megan

Stella Etc.

"Super-sweet and cool as an ice-cream"
Mizz magazine

SCHOLASTIC

Scholastic Children's Books
An imprint of Scholastic Ltd
Euston House, 24 Eversholt Street
London, NW1 1DB, UK
Registered office: Westfield Road, Southam, Warwickshire, CV47 0RA
SCHOLASTIC and associated logos are trademarks and/or registered trademarks
of Scholastic Inc.

First published in the UK by Scholastic Ltd, 2005
This edition published in the UK by Scholastic Ltd, 2010

Text copyright © Karen McCombie, 2005
The right of Karen McCombie to be identified as the author of this work
has been asserted by her.

ISBN 978 1407 11779 9

Printed in the UK by CPI Bookmarque, Croydon, Surrey.
Papers used by Scholastic Children's Books are made from wood grown in
sustainable forests.

3 5 7 9 10 8 6 4 2

www.scholastic.co.uk/zone

Contents

From: *stella*
To: Frankie
Subject:
Attachments:

Hi Frankie!

How're you doing? I'm prettY @^$*^^****************************0000 000))))))))))))))))))))))))))))))))))))000000000000 0000000000000000000000000000000000@

From: *stella*
To: Frankie
Subject: Whoops!
Attachments: Truly, madly Megan

Sorry about that e-mail you just got, Frankie!

Hope you didn't think I'd gone completely insane (bet you were worried that all the salty seaside air here had fuzzed up my brain!).

Blame my weird cat instead – I'd just written you this great long e-mail and was about to attach the, er, attachment, when Peaches jumped on the desk, walked all over the keyboard – deleting what I'd keyed in and tapping

1

some random rubbish of his own – and somehow managed to *send* the blimmin' thing.

Y'know, Peaches is definitely getting spookier. I had this dream last night that I was living back in London, and hanging out with you and the girls again. But I couldn't hear what any of you were saying, 'cause your voices were being drowned out by this loud sort of *humming* sound. Then I woke up to find Peaches sitting on my chest, practically nose-to-nose, staring hard at me and purring his head off. I *swear* it was like he wasn't just reading my mind, but sneaking into my dreams too. . .

OK, admit it – now you really *do* think the salty seaside air has fuzzed up my brain, don't you?!

Got to go (before I say anything else mad!), 'cause I promised Megan I'd e-mail her a photo of the time she was modelling in the leopard-skin dress and tea-cosy hat.

Uh-oh . . . that sounds stunningly mad, doesn't it? Well, just read the attachment and you'll see that it's not. *Much*. . .

Miss you ☹, but M8s 4eva ☺!

stella

PS Maybe Peaches was typing in code. Maybe @

2

^ $* ^ ^ ****************************OOOOOO
O))))))))))))))))))))))))))))))))))OOOOOOOOOOOOO
OOOOOOOOOOOOOOOOOOOOOOOOOOOOOOOO@ means "helloooooooooooooooo from Peaches". Or maybe not. . .

Chapter 1

A whiff, an oink and a splat

It couldn't last long; being relaxed, I mean. Not with a dog that farts in its sleep.

"What's that stink?" asked Rachel, wrinkling up her pretty nose, and looking around the beach for a mountain of rotting seaweed or whatever else might be causing the current whiff.

"Sorry – it's cat food," said TJ with a shrug.

Rachel looked confused, but then she'd only been best friends with me and TJ for a week, and didn't know us – or Bob the dog's occasional bottom problems – very well yet.

"TJ's local corner shop only sells cat food," I started to explain, gazing at the hairy Alsatian sprawled out and snoring like a living shaggy rug on the sand next to us. "And if TJ's mum forgets to buy dog biscuits at the supermarket, then they have to feed Bob cat food. Which gives him the . . . er . . . *problem* you can smell."

I didn't want to say the "fart" word out

5

loud – not when my two-and-a-bit-year-old twin brothers were within earshot. I didn't want to spoil a lovely, lazy, sunny morning by having Jake and Jamie parroting "FARTFARTFARTFART FART!!" at the top of their voices. . .

"Yewww!" mumbled Rachel, wafting her hand under her nose.

Out of the corner of my eye, I spotted Ellie – TJ's kid sister – suddenly start fanning herself in the same way. In between building sand-castles and singing annoying nursery rhymes with my brothers, she'd had her eyes totally glued to Rachel. I was pretty sure there was a serious case of hero worship developing there. If you were five, thirteen-year-old Rachel must look like the most gorgeous, grown-up girl in the world. Mind you, *I* was thirteen and thought much the same. . .

"Here, have a sniff of that – it'll take your mind off the pong!" TJ grinned, lungeing towards Rachel, holding one of his kicked-off trainers.

(TJ got a real buzz from teasing Rach – not so long ago she'd been part of a bitchy little clique who gave him a hard time, and he hadn't been friends with her long enough to completely forgive her *just* yet. . .)

"Gerroff!! God, why do boys have to be so horrible?" groaned Rachel, ducking back out of smelly-trainer range.

"They're just born that way, they can't help it, the poor things!" I grinned, earning a smelly trainer in my lap as punishment.

"Y'know, speaking of how horrible boys can be, my brother is such a *pig*!" Rachel suddenly moaned, leaning her arms back in the sand and lazily watching the arc of the trainer as I chucked it *way* over TJ's head to safety.

"How come?" I asked.

Now I spotted something *else* out of the corner of my eye . . . when Rachel spoke just now, Jake and Jamie glanced at each other and started to giggle. Which is always a worrying sign.

"Well, last night I went into his room and—"

"Oink!"

"Oink, oink!"

"Jake. . . Jamie. . . Shut up, please – Rachel is talking," I warned them sternly. "Carry on, Rachel."

"Yeah, go on!" said TJ. "I'm *dying* to hear why you think Si is such a pig!"

"Oink! Oink! Hee, hee, hee!" giggled Jake.

"Oi—"

Before Jamie could properly join in with the barnyard noises again, I slapped my hand across his mouth.

"Sorry, Rachel," I mumbled. "Hey, *yuck*!! That is *disgusting*, Jamie!"

Quickly, I grabbed my drooled-on hand away from Jamie's grinning face, and scrambled about in my skirt pocket for a tissue.

"OINK!" yelled Jamie, now that his mouth had been liberated.

Of course, Jake couldn't be outdone like that.

"OINK!OINK!OINK!OINK!OINK!OINK! OINK. . ."

Good grief.

It was Monday, the start of my fourth week in my new home town of Portbay. My parents decided to drag our family here from London because they said stuff about us all having "a better quality of life" in this super-sleepy seaside town. Well, OK, I guess it *was* pretty nice to spend a summery Monday morning sitting on a sunny beach like I was doing right now. But the only way my "quality of life" could *really* be improved was if Mum and Dad had decided to leave the twins behind in London when we moved. (Only joking. Kind of.)

". . .OINK!OINK!OINK!OINK. . ."

"Stella, will I take them away to play?" asked Ellie, scrambling to her feet.

I could have kissed her.

Ellie was sometimes tiringly bouncy, and her habit of bursting into song or tap-dancing on the slightest hard surface could drive you mad. But she really was a nice, thoughtful little kid. I hoped the twins would outgrow this drooling/biting/roaring/wrecking phase they were going through and start acting more like Ellie soon, but I can't say I held out much hope for that.

"Yes, please!" I half-said, half-sighed in relief.

Me, TJ and Rachel stayed silent, till Ellie grabbed hands with Jake and Jamie and waddled them – still oinking – a little way along the beach, where the boys immediately began entertaining themselves by kicking down the big, ornate sandcastle some kid had lovingly built and left behind.

"So, you were saying . . . *why* exactly is Si supposed to be a pig?" asked TJ.

Ellie might be showing signs of hero-worshipping Rachel, but I had a sneaking suspicion that TJ ever-so-slightly hero-worshipped her big brother Simon. And just like Ellie, I could understand why. Si might look a little on the scary side with his pierced lip and black eyeliner, but he was also frighteningly cool and spookily handsome (yeah, even *with* the lip-ring and eyeliner). And he happened to have a summer job in The Vault, TJ's favourite shop in town. It was this dark, dingy and very hip CD and comic store in a back lane off the high street; the sort of place you suspected you could stumble upon really rare records and plague germs in the darkest, dustiest, unswept corners.

"Well, I was forced to go in his pit of a room last night to find the hairdryer," Rachel started up her story again, "and when I bent down to pick it up off the floor, I saw all this *stuff* under his bed!"

"Stuff?" I asked nervously, not exactly sure what seventeen-year-old boys kept under their beds.

"Plates – loads of plates with old, dried-up mouldy bits of pizza and food on them!" Rachel said with a grimace. "*And* wrinkled piles of smelly socks!"

"Gross!" I mumbled.

TJ, meanwhile, just sniggered a bit. Did he have the odd half-a-sandwich and lost sock under his bed too?

"I don't know how Si gets so many girls crawling after him," said Rachel, rolling her eyes. "He's such a freak. But they all have crushes on him – specially that weirdo Tilda."

Urgh . . . there was a funny mix of feelings in my chest just then – when Rachel was calling people "freaks" and "weirdos", I mean. I know I used those words too, but not with that particular flip, nasty tone in my voice. I guess what bothered me most was that Rachel and her old crew made me feel pretty much like a freak and a weirdo during my first couple of weeks here in Portbay, with their stares and sarky digs.

But then again, I was quite up for hearing more about Tilda. I'd seen her wandering round town on her own a lot, in this bizarro arty outfit of black leather jacket, pink tutu, stripy tights and Doc Marten boots.

"Tilda's all right," shrugged TJ. "I think she's kind of cute, in a . . . a . . ."

"In a weirdo way!" Rachel finished his sentence for him. "Well, she's freaky enough for my brother, but he just can't see it. Keeps saying they're just mates, but she follows him round all over the place like a lovesick puppy. Or looking the way she does, she's more like a lovesick *bat* or something. . ."

PARP!! PARP!!

Call me naïve, but you don't really expect

to hear old-fashioned bicycle horns on a beach. Specially not directly in your ear. Which is why the three of us (and Bob) nearly jumped out of our skin/fur.

But then as soon as we saw the pair of clowns looming over us – all red noses and painted-on grins – we relaxed.

At least, me and TJ did.

"Hi John! Hi Bev!" TJ grinned up at them.

"Hey, call us the Mystic Marzipans while we're on duty!" the woman clown smiled back his way.

PARP!! PARP!! PARP!! PARP!! parped John/Mr Mystic Marzipan.

Rachel looked as confused as when TJ had come out with the cat-food comment earlier.

"I already told you about Mr and Mrs Mystic Marzipan, Rachel – they're my sort-of neighbours, remember?" I said, trying to jog her memory. "They're renting the holiday cottage over the alley from us. They're doing lots of, er, *stuff* for the Portbay Gala Week."

"We're performing in various capacities, that's correct!" Bev/Mrs Mystic Marzipan nodded at both me and Rachel, making her pink, wiggy head of curls bob back and forth. "And who might *you* be?"

Rachel seemed to be finding it difficult to answer a question addressed by a clown (maybe she was transfixed by the flashing red nose?) so I answered on her behalf.

"This is our friend, Rachel!"

"Pleased to meet you, Rachel," said Mrs Mystic Marzipan, holding a hand out to her.

Rachel warily went to shake it – but ended up finding a paper flower placed between her fingers as if by magic. And there was *more*.

"If you look in the front pocket of your bag, dear, you'll find there's some info on *all* the events taking place during the Gala week."

"Thanks. . ." mumbled Rachel, plucking one of Mrs Mystic Marzipan's leaflets from the front pouch of her pink vinyl rucksack.

"Right, better get on – got plenty of these to hand out!" said Mrs Mystic Marzipan, clutching a fat bundle of leaflets and following after her husband, who'd run up PARPing at the squealing, giggling bunch of kids along the beach, who just happened to be my brothers and Ellie.

"Those people are *weird*. . ." mumbled Rachel.

"Those people are *brilliant*!" TJ laughed. "They taught me how to juggle and everything!"

Rachel didn't look convinced, as if TJ had

just tried to tell her tomato sauce on ice-cream was a great idea. But I'd got too sidetracked by something I'd just noticed to join in and argue about why Mr and Mrs Marzipan were absolutely as cool as ketchup.

"'*Search for a Gala Princess*!'" I read out from the top of a list on the leaflet in Rachel's hand.

(The rest of the list waffled on about bouncy castles, art exhibitions, puppet shows, plays and a parade on Saturday morning – which would feature, it said, the Gala Princess.)

Don't get me wrong; I wasn't all *excited* about the idea of a Gala Princess competition. After all, I was pretty sure that *I* had about as much chance of being picked to be Gala Princess as a snowball had of staying in one piece in a pizza oven. But reading it just got me imagining the sensation of being stared at by the whole of the town, not to mention heaps of holidaymakers. The very notion of it made every shy molecule in my body (and trust me, I have a kerzillion of 'em) completely *cringe*.

Who'd be confident enough about the way they looked to stand up to *that* kind of attention? (Not to mention all that ogling. . .)

As soon as that thought *ping*ed into my head, I found myself gazing at Rachel, and saw that TJ was doing the same. Well, she *was* the prettiest teenager in Portbay (and she knew it), so who else could be the Gala Princess?

"No way! Don't look at *me*!" Rachel suddenly shook her head hard. "It's bad enough having a seizure in front of a café full of people – I don't exactly fancy falling flat on my face in front of the whole town!"

I could see why Rachel was nervous. She'd only just found out she was epileptic, and hadn't exactly enjoyed the couple of shaking, twitching, fainting fits she'd had so far – once at the outdoor swimming pool and once halfway through a song on the karaoke machine at the Shingles café.

"How about this, then?" said TJ, about to read something else he'd spotted on the flyer. "'*Talent Show – show us your talents and win a fantastic prize! First round: Tuesday, 10 a.m., The Sea Stage. . .*'"

"The Sea Stage?" said Rachel, crinkling up her nose. "Is that what they're putting up along there?"

Before Bob's botty problem had distracted us, we'd been lazily watching a bunch of guys erecting some kind of wide, wooden platform further along the sands. Mind you, we hadn't been that curious about it up till now, since it hadn't been as much fun to watch as the slowly inflating bouncy castle up at the beach car park.

"S'pose it is," I said with a shrug. "Hey, Rachel – you could do your Kylie song again!"

Yesterday afternoon at the Shingles café, Rachel had managed to put seizures to the back of her mind and made it all the way through "Can't Get You Out of my Head", and at the end of it got a standing ovation (instead of a ride in an ambulance, like the first time she'd tried it).

"Not sure if I'd risk it . . . and I can't do it anyway," mumbled Rachel, staring down at the leaflet while idly fixing the paper flower Mrs Mystic Marzipan had magicked up into her long, dark hair. "Mum's made an appointment for me tomorrow morning with the doctor."

Eek . . . *that* wasn't going to be much fun. Especially when it meant that Rachel was going to have to confess her little secret to the doctor; i.e., her little secret about—

"Uh-oh . . . *whoahhhhh!*" I heard TJ say, *just* before I got splatted sideways – and ended up with a face full of beach.

"Oops! God, I'm SOOO sorry!" said someone.

Blinking sand from my eyelashes, I raised

16

my head just enough to see a gangly teenage girl with blonde-ish hair smiling awkwardly down at me.

Then the strangest thing happened – she was all of a sudden upside down.

And then the right way up again.

And then upside down again.

And the right way up again.

And she was getting smaller and smaller all the time. . .

Why did I feel like I was starring in *Alice in Wonderland*? Did I have concussion?!

"Hey, well done, Stella!" said TJ, as he helped me sit up. "You are officially the first person I've ever met who's been the victim of a hit-and-run cartwheel!"

Hit-and-run cartwheel?! I thought dizzily, as I tried to focus on the girl spiralling along the beach away from us.

"Maybe she should try walking, like a normal person," grumbled Rachel, staring hard after her too.

"Or wear L-plates?!" laughed TJ, rubbing my hair so hard to get the sand out of it that I felt dizzier than ever.

Help, I think I needed to sit down, if I wasn't sitting down already. . .

Chapter 2

"Everybodywantstobeacat!!"

It's funny how my brothers can be maddeningly wide awake when I'd prefer them to be comatose, and then comatose when it would be kind of *fun* for them to be awake.

"Hey, Jake! Jamie! You're missing the balloon animals!" I called down to them snoozling in their buggy.

Nothing.

And they weren't just missing out on the balloon animals (being squidged and twisted together by none other than Mr and Mrs Mystic Marzipan), but all the other acts dotted along the prom for Gala Week too.

"Here, Stella," said Mum, appearing at the side of the parked buggy, with a double-scoop ice-cream cone each for me and her. "Got pistachio and vanilla, or strawberry and vanilla. Which one d'you want?"

My brain can play the strangest tricks on me . . .

the tiniest thing can get me instantly thinking about stuff that seems totally unconnected. Like cut grass; that always reminds me of my old friend Parminder, 'cause of this one time me and her and Frankie and the others had a grass fight up at Hampstead Heath and Parminder accidentally ended up with a *worm* – as well as grass – down her top. Then there's Ribena; that reminds me of my Auntie V (for Vanessa), not 'cause she ever drinks the stuff but because she lives in this all-white flat, and my earliest memory of visiting her was squishing a carton of Ribena too hard and landing a splodge of ominous purple on her pale as milk carpet. . .

"I'll have the strawberry and vanilla, thanks," I answered Mum, still mulling over how the pistachio, strawberry and vanilla of the ice-cream reminded me of Mrs Sticky Toffee, the old lady I kept bumping into around and about Portbay. I'd always spot her, in her light green raincoat and a funny pink hat, swinging her tiny, shiny cream handbag that was permanently stuffed with toffees. (That's where the nickname I'd given her came from. I still didn't know her *real* name, but then she didn't know mine. She could be Mrs Elsie Spam and I could be Hermione Doolittle for all either of us knew. . .)

"So the boys are still zonked, are they?"

"Totally out of it!" I nodded at Mum, quickly shaking the hideously ridiculous idea of being called Hermione Doolittle out of my head.

As I spoke, I glanced down at the top of two toddler heads; one with spiky fair hair and one with a mop of reddish-blond curls (the twins weren't what you could call identical).

"So what do you reckon to *that*?" asked Mum, nodding to a young bloke dressed all in black with a white painted face. Two crystal balls were slithering and sliding up and down his arms and across his shoulders like they were big, round dollops of molten metal. With a slight arm flick here and a shrug of the shoulder there, he made the bodily loop-de-loop look totally effortless.

"Pretty good," I nodded, wondering how on earth you find out that you're good at something like loop-de-looping crystal balls around your body. Try mentioning *that* to your career teacher at school. ("You want to be a crystal ball loop-de-looper? Er, have you thought about computing instead?")

"Not so sure about the human statue though. . ." Mum whispered sideways to me.

"Oh yeah! Isn't the point of being a human statue to stay as *still* as a statue?" I whispered back, gazing through my sunshades at the guy in the suit and top hat all spray-painted silver.

He seemed to be fidgeting a lot and blinking hard. In fact, he was blinking upwards – at the sun, I thought at first. And then I spotted a seagull swooping in a lazy figure of eight *right* above his head.

"*CAWWWW*!" the bird squawked at me as we made eye contact.

Ah, it was TJ's ex-stalker seagull, the one that used to dive-bomb him till he fed it and made friends. Looked like it was doing a little freelance stalking just for fun. Or maybe it could smell the human statue's packed lunch.

"Oh dear . . . I hope Jake and Jamie wake up in time for the talent show, or they'll miss seeing Ellie doing her turn!" said Mum, still glancing down at the flopped-out, non-matching bundles of boy in the buggy.

Oh, yeah, Ellie's "turn". TJ said she'd been driving him mad with it. For the last twenty-four hours – ever since she'd looked at the leaflet handed out by the Mystic Marzipans – Ellie had been in a tap-dancing frenzy, belting out all the songs in her five-year-old repertoire (anything from "Twinkle, Twinkle Little Star" to Britney Spears's "Oops! I Did It Again", to a jingle she'd heard on an ad for multi-vitamins, apparently).

"Pity your friend Rachel isn't performing," Mum carried on. "After you going on about her voice I'd have loved to hear her sing."

"Well, I think she'd rather be here singing than at the doctor's, telling him she lied!" I said.

This epilepsy thing of Rachel's . . . the specialist at the hospital had been trying to figure out how she'd developed it all of a sudden. One thing he'd gone on about was that it *might* be linked to her periods starting (in a very *teeny* number of girls, that can be what the doctor bloke called a "trigger"). But Rachel's mum had dived right in and said that couldn't be possible, since Rach had started her periods a whole year earlier.

Except oops! she *hadn't*. Rachel's horrible ex-friends Kayleigh, Hazel and Brooke had made her so completely paranoid about being "late" starting the whole period thing that she pretended it had already happened for her.

Then *blam!*, she found herself lumped with this big, fat fib that she didn't know how to get rid of. . .

"Was her mother all right about it when Rachel finally told her on Sunday?" asked Mum.

Sunday: the day Rachel's periods really DID start. And the day she realized she'd have to come clean with everyone. ("Well, it's hardly *everyone*, is it?" I'd told her when we stood outside her mum's shop, while she geared herself up to go in and admit to her lie. "It's your mum and the doctor, that's all!" "Yeah, it's not like it'll make front page news in the local paper!" TJ had chipped in, even though he was supposed to be standing a discreet few feet away out of listening range while we talked over the delicate-ish subject.)

"Rachel said her mum was fine about it," I shrugged. "She said the thing that confused her mum the most was what Rachel was doing with all the Kotex stuff she was buying her every month."

"And what *was* she doing with it all?" Mum asked, her eyebrows raised in befuddlement.

Don't know *what* Mum was imagining. That Rachel was making a modern art sculpture of a giant *shoe* or something out of sanitary towels maybe. . .?

"She kept all the unopened packets in the back of her wardrobe," I explained, putting Mum out of her misery (or at least her befuddlement).

"Ladies and gentleman! Boys and girls! Are you ready to see a fantastic show of talent today?" a voice suddenly boomed through a nearby tannoy, putting an end to our current discussion.

(Poor Rachel – she'd *die* of embarrassment if she knew me and my mum were chatting about her like this. . .)

"Uh-oh – it's starting already!" I said to Mum over the roar of "YESSSS!"s coming from the crowd lazing down on the beach in front of the makeshift stage.

"I'll have to watch it from here – we'll never get the buggy down on to the sands while the boys are conked out. But look – there's TJ waving to you. Go on; he's saved you a place!"

With a quick wave to Mum, I skipped down the few steps that led directly on to the sands and began the tricky task of stepping and wobbling my way through the packed, seated audience till I got to TJ and Bob.

Much to the annoyance of everyone sardined around, TJ had got his pooch to sprawl out – doing his excellent rug imitation – so there was plenty of space for me to sit in once Bob had huffed his hairy self upright.

"Want some?" I asked, offering my ice-cream

to TJ.

"Thanks," said TJ, taking it from me quickly before Bob did more than just sniff at it.

"Where's Ellie?"

"Over at the side of the stage, waiting to go on. Mum's with her."

"How's she doing?" I asked, straining and failing to catch sight of Ellie – and Mrs O'Connell – in a queue of "talented" performers by the side of the stage.

"Mum? Oh, she's OK – just a bit nervous." TJ grinned, deliberately misunderstanding me.

"*Ellie*. I mean how's *Ellie*!"

"Well, she was so excited she forgot to *breathe* when she was practising her song this morning. She got to the second last line and had to stop and pant like crazy! Freaked Bob out a bit though; he thought there was another dog in the hou—"

TJ ground to a halt as the bloke on stage – who looked kind of familiar – cheerfully asked for silence.

And for most of the time through the next five acts, me and TJ *were* more or less silent . . . if you don't count the stifled giggles, the whispered comments and then the huge cheers and claps we gave them all.

"The girl who could play the recorder through her left nostril was *definitely* the best up till now," I told TJ.

"Are we talking best? Or best at being *worst*?" TJ checked with me.

"Um . . . both. They're all pretty terrible, aren't they?" I giggled.

Yep, it was a case of so far, so bad, but in the most entertaining way. Not only was there the girl who could play the recorder through one side of her nose, but then there were the three white lads in their twenties trying (and failing) to rap, a pudgy woman who could make her ears waggle (we just had to believe that since we couldn't see it from where we were sitting), a kid who told jokes that weren't technically jokes (i.e. they weren't funny) and an old guy who yodelled his way through "Danny Boy" (spotted Mum up on the prom with a tissue when he came on – was she having a sniffle or stifling a giggle too?).

I think everyone in the ever-growing crowd thought the same as me and TJ; that this rubbish was *excellent* fun and everyone deserved plenty of whooping and encouragement.

Especially the *next* act. . .

"Whoah! *What* is she wearing?!" I asked TJ,

once I'd whooped and clapped Ellie's entrance on stage.

"Everything. She couldn't choose," muttered TJ.

Ellie's outfit started well, if you looked at her from the feet up, and then steadily got more bizarre. I mean, the tap shoes and lacy ankle socks were fine, but teamed with a fairy costume, including wings, a stripy T-shirt, a feather boa and a pair of glittery deelyboppers jammed on her head and the whole look made me sort of *dizzy*.

"Hello, little lady!" boomed the bloke with the mike. "And what's *your* name?"

"But you *know* what my name is, Mr Harper!"

The mike bloke, or Mr Harper, or whatever . . . it had slowly dawned on me who he was. He worked at Portbay library, and taught kids – like Ellie – to tap dance. When I last saw him he was putting books back on the library shelves while humming a tune and tippety-tap-dancing along the library's shiny lino floor. (If you hadn't noticed already, Portbay is wall-to-wall full of slightly strange people. OK, nutters. But *nice* nutters.)

"Yes, I *know* I know your name," Mr Harper said patiently to Ellie. "But you need to tell the lovely ladies and gentlemen and boys and girls what it is!"

"Oh. My name is Electra Z O'Connell," Ellie answered very formally (though it's kind of hard to look formal when you're wearing the entire contents of a dressing-up box).

"Right then, Electra," Mr Harper continued, "and what might you be doing for us today?"

"Singin' and dancin'."

"OK. . . Right, ladies and gentlemen, boys and girls, let's have some shush while Electra does some singing and dancing!"

With a wave of Mr Harper's arms, and a dazzling smile from Ellie, the performance began. It was pretty good, but I think nerves got the better of TJ's little sis. From what I remembered of it, "Everybody Wants to be a Cat" from Disney's *Aristocats* movie actually lasts two or three minutes, but Ellie did a hyper-speed version that she raced through in about twenty seconds. Her feet were flying in a frenzied tapping blur as they struggled to keep up with her hurriedly squeaked vocal. She looked just about ready to faint from lack of oxygen by the end (for the second time today), but there was a HUGE beam on her face as everyone cheered like crazy for her.

And the cheering was just as warm for the next

act. Well, perhaps it was just as warm from the *rest* of the locals and holidaymakers in the audience – with the exception of me and TJ.

Y'see, me and TJ, we had our own reasons for *not* cheering on this particular girl. . .

"Urgh . . . didn't know *she* was going to be in the competition," grumbled TJ, as Rachel's ex-best mate Kayleigh came strutting on stage. "What's her talent? Being a total $?%!!?"

Sorry, I had to censor what TJ said, as it was very, very rude. And I know it might sound a pretty *strong* thing to say, but Kayleigh really was a bit of a $?%!!. How else could you describe someone who is *mortified* when their supposed best friend has a seizure, instead of *sorry* for her? And what kind of best friend ditches their mate when they're ill? Kayleigh, that's who.

"What's with her clothes?" I wondered aloud.

"*What* clothes?" said TJ, who – like me – was wincing at the sight of Kayleigh's sequinned Union Jack bikini top, minuscule denim cut-off shorts and red bandana tied around her *thigh*.

"D'you think she's trying to look like a backing dancer off an MTV video or something?" I suggested.

"She looks more like the back of a bus. . ."

mumbled TJ darkly.

It wasn't strictly true; Kayleigh was quite a pretty girl, but meanness was written all over her face, which kind of blotted out the prettiness, if you see what I mean. And she *did* look like she'd got dressed in the dark, or for a bet today. . .

I'd been lost in thoughts of how on earth Kayleigh could think she looked good in that outfit and managed to miss what Mr Harper was saying as he introduced her. Before I got the chance to ask TJ for a quick catch-up, Kayleigh pushed a control on the boom-box she'd brought out on stage with her, and the whole audience were instantly deafened by. . .

"That's that Kylie song! The one that Rachel always sings!" I yelled in TJ's direction, over the top of Bob's twitching ears.

"Huh? But why would Kayleigh go and nick the same song?!" TJ shouted back, his brown hair flopping across the frown lines on his forehead.

Exactly what *I* was thinking. Kayleigh could have chosen one of a zillion other hit songs. Even a zillion other hit songs by Kylie Minogue. So why *that* one?

Maybe 'cause it was one of her favourites, same as her (very recently) ex-best friend Rachel?

Maybe 'cause she had no brain of her own, and chose it since she'd heard Rachel sing it so well?

Or maybe it was 'cause Rachel had had such a great response the one-and-a-half times she'd sung it at the Shingles café, and Kayleigh wanted to be just as successful? If that was the case, then what Kayleigh seemed to be missing was the fact that Rachel was a brilliant singer, and Kayleigh, er, *wasn't*.

And no amount of bad dance moves, skimpy outfits and bum wiggling could cover *that* up. . .

"Do you s'pose Kayleigh actually thinks she looks *gorgeous*?" sniggered TJ all of a sudden.

"I guess so – and so do *they*!" I said, nudging TJ to turn and check out the wolf-whistling bunch of idiots on the edge of the crowd. It was Sam's gang: four of the most obnoxious boys you could hope (or dread) to meet. They were hanging out with Hazel and Brooke, who were whoo-hooing their mate Kayleigh for all they were worth.

"Yeah, but remember – the whole lot of them have only got about thirteen brain cells put together, so they'd probably find a *wheelie* bin gorgeous if it was wearing a bikini top. . ."

TJ gave Bob's head a comforting scratch – Kayleigh's screeching was obviously unsettling him;

31

his ears were practically swivelling like helicopter propellers. And above all the bass-thumping and warbling from the stage I could *definitely* hear a distinctly unhappy whine.

"It'll be all over soon," I muttered to Bob, offering him the wafer end of my cone to take his doggy mind off the racket on stage.

And sure enough, with a final, badly out of tune note and a wiggle of her bum, Kayleigh's talent spot (thankfully) ended. And just like all the other performers, she got a chorus of cheers and hurrays. OK, well, maybe not from *us*. . .

"That was a very, um, spirited performance from Kayleigh!" said Mr Harper, bounding back on to the stage. "And now for the last entrant in today's heat. . . Come here, dear! Now tell everyone your name!"

A blonde-ish-haired, bright-eyed, skinny teenage girl awkwardly shuffled towards centre stage, dressed in kind of tomboyish shorts and a baggy T-shirt.

She leaned *way* too close to the microphone and the name "MEGAN. MEGAN SAMSON!" blasted out as a loud, distorted boom.

"Hey, Stella – that's the girl who cartwheeled into you!" said TJ.

"So she is!" I nodded, tilting my head a little to picture her more from the squint angle I'd seen her at yesterday.

"OK!" laughed Mr Harper. "And do you live around here, Megan, or are you on holiday?"

"I'M ON HOLIDAY," she boomed again, till Mr Harper motioned her to stand back a bit, "with my mum and my dad and my sister – we're staying at the Seaview Holiday Park!"

With that, the girl turned and pointed up at the collection of ugly-bug caravans perched up on the rocky headland to the left of the beach. They ruined the view whether you were frowning at them from Portbay, or scowling at them from Sugar Bay cove on the other side of the headland.

"Super. And are you having a good holiday so far?"

"Er . . . kind of!" the girl shrugged, shoving her hands deep into her shorts pockets and wrinkling her nose.

It wasn't the bright and breezy answer Mr Harper had expected, I didn't think, and he seemed thrown for a second.

"And are your family here in the audience to support you?" he tried to bluster on with a bit of casual banter.

"NOPE," said the girl, forgetting herself and leaning too close to the microphone again.

I could hear some nasty laughing over by the edge of the crowd. No prizes guessing where *that* was coming from. Specially since Sam and Hazel and Brooke and that lot had been joined by Kayleigh, fresh from her "star" turn.

"Oh. . . OK. Well, um, how about you tell us what your act is?"

"ACROBATICS."

"Right then, Megan. . . Off you go!"

Before Mr Harper had even finished his sentence and backed away, Megan threw herself with a thump into something that I *think* is called a backward crab (and would be called "ouch!" if *I* tried it). Then she sort of *threw* her legs in the air and ended up walking about the stage on her hands for what seemed like *ages*.

It was the sort of thing that maybe looks impressive at the Olympics, with girls in sporty leotards flipping elegantly around to fancy classical music, but this Megan girl was more gawky than elegant, loudly panting her way around the stage while her T-shirt slowly slouched down towards her waist. From where I was sitting, it seemed like she was in serious danger of revealing her bra to the world, which made me *wince* with worry for her.

But then – *thunk*! – she whirled herself from a handstand into a cartwheel or three. She might have cartwheeled herself right off of the stage, if it wasn't for the fact that she clattered straight into Mr Harper and used him like a human crash barrier.

"Ooooff!" he grunted into the mike. "Uh . . . big round of applause, please, for Megan!"

Megan straightened her gangly self up, pushed the mop of messy blondey hair from her face and beamed happily, as the crowd did its usual roar of encouragement.

And then her smile faded, as the sound of boos sank in. . .

"YAY!" I yelled, slapping my hands even more loudly together.

"Hurray!!!" yelled TJ. Like me, he was doing his best to drown out the booing coming from Sam and Kayleigh's crew too.

At that point, I glanced up at Mum on the prom, to see if she'd registered the rudeness as well. Weirdly, she was looking straight at me, like she'd been trying to get my attention. And it wasn't to pull faces in Kayleigh and Sam's direction – she was frantically pointing at something further along the prom.

A *ginger* something.

"It's Peaches!" Mum seemed to be mouthing in surprise.

Ah, Peaches. Peaches had adopted us about half-a-second after we moved to Portbay. Apart from fur and purring, he didn't have much in common with your average cat. For a start, this strange scent of peaches and cream wafted after him wherever he went (pretty bizarre for such a fat, battle-scarred scruffbucket). Then there was his habit of turning up miles from home (did he take the bus?). And that wasn't even *starting* on his general spookiness.

And right now, his spooky green gaze was fixed firmly on the blondey girl slinking shame-facedly off stage . . . except there was an arm barring her from slinking anywhere. Not that she saw it, so went clunking chest-first into Mr Harper.

"Oops-a-daisy, there!" he said, regaining his feet. "Can you just wait here, please, Megan? And could all the other contestants gather on the stage too? The audience will be voting for their winner any second now!"

"There's Ellie!" I nudged TJ, spying his little sis break away from her mum and run so fast that the sparkly ping-pong balls on the end of her deelyboppers bounced wildly.

"What's she *like*?" TJ sniggered affectionately. "But look – check out Kayleigh!"

And so I checked her out, and spotted Rachel's former friend stepping daintily over arms and legs and knees as she made her way back to the stage, smiling her crocodile smile and waving at everyone as she went.

"She's acting like she thinks she's won!" I muttered, clocking the smug expression.

"Well, she's in for a shock," TJ muttered back. "It doesn't matter how 'gorgeous' she tried to be, the whole audience isn't *deaf*. They know that the only way her voice would be bearable was if she took that stupid scarf off her leg and tied it round her *gob*!"

Uh-oh – I could hardly hear him all of a sudden: Mr Harper was holding his hand above the head of the girl who played the recorder with her left nostril and the crowd were going nuts.

In fact, the crowd went nuts for *everyone*, as Mr Harper walked along the line of wannabe winners.

Peaches, I noticed, didn't flicker an ear at the deafening noise. He looked on with a completely unreadable, or possibly bored gaze, until Mr

Harper said, "Megan!" and then his long tail flipped over the edge of the prom and flickered back and forward agitatedly.

What was that all about?

"Well, at the end of the voting procedure, ladies and gentlemen, boys and girls, I judge the winner to be. . ." Mr Harper bellowed into the microphone, then paused for effect, ". . .Electra O'Connell!"

I think Mr Harper began blustering on about Ellie going through to Friday's final alongside the winners from the next two days' heats, but me and TJ weren't listening properly, since we were *way* too busy yelling ourselves hoarse.

Judging by the volume of cheering going on, the rest of the audience seemed as chuffed with the result as us. Ellie might have sounded like a tape that was stuck on fast-forward when she sang, but she was just so ridiculously cute that no one else on stage seemed to mind that she'd won.

No one except a frosty-faced girl with her arms crossed defensively across her Union Jack bikini top. . .

Chapter 3

Sing-along-a-bribe...

From where I was standing, Mrs O'Connell looked like an old-fashioned deckchair.

I don't mean that she had legs like chunks of wood or anything; she just had on this long, stripy, hippyish dress that flapped in the sea breeze.

"Your mum must be pretty proud of Ellie," I said, as me and TJ waited for Mrs O'Connell to finish chatting to Mr Harper. She was holding on tight to Ellie's hand, but since she was off to direct some drama group rehearsal this afternoon, we were expecting Ellie to come running our way at any second, deelyboppers boinging and fairy-dress fluttering.

"Hmm... I don't know if Mum's *proud*, exactly. Not the way normal parents are proud of their kids," muttered TJ.

"How d'you mean?" I asked.

"Well, I bet she's already given Ellie a lecture about her breathing and singing technique. And she'll be quizzing Mr Harper about the tap-dancing; getting him to give Ellie extra lessons before the talent show final on Friday afternoon or something. . ."

TJ didn't need to explain any more. I'd heard all about stage mums; my Auntie V is an actors' agent and deliberately doesn't represent children 'cause she says for every sane parent out there, there's some bossy dragon practically prodding their little darling on to the stage with sharp sticks in search of fame. And as Mrs O'Connell was one of those actors who never made the big-time and seemed ever so slightly bitter about it, she was probably desperate for her one "talented" child (i.e. Ellie) to be a success.

Meanwhile, "regular" TJ practically always got lumbered with being Ellie's permanent babysitter whenever their mum was busy, which was *most* of the time.

"She's given me some tickets, by the way."

I didn't know what TJ was on about. My face must have said "Huh?" pretty clearly, 'cause he went on to explain himself. Sort of.

"For *The Roar of the Rainforest*: the show Mum's directing all this week, for the Gala. She's given me some free tickets to go see it tomorrow night at the town hall. Should be awful. Fancy it?"

"You bet!" I grinned, knowing that I could bank on having a good time at even the most awful event if I was with TJ.

"Uh-oh. . . Ellie's been set free – here she comes!" laughed TJ, watching as his sis came hurtling barefoot across the hot sands, her tap shoes and lacy socks presumably tucked away inside her Bang On The Door bag.

"Where are Jake and Jamie? Did they see me singing?" she panted, joining us as we turned and headed towards Rachel's mum's arty-crafty gift shop, where we were going to meet Rach after her doctor's appointment.

"Um . . . yes," I lied, not wanting to disappoint Ellie or burst her winner's bubble. "But they were really tired, so Mum had to take them home for their nap."

That part was true at least; Mum and the boys *had* headed back to our house, where they'd wake up either because they weren't tired any more, or 'cause Dad was sledgehammering another poor, defenceless wall of our cottage into smithereens. (The house was looking like a cross between a building site and the pages of some fancy homes magazine right now. During Dad's DIY-athon,

Mum was desperately trying to make the place look cosy by chucking pretty throws over piles of tools and sticking big vases of flowers in front of bare brickwork. Dad had promised Mum that he'd have the building work finished by the end of summer. The only thing is, I saw that he had his fingers crossed behind his back when he was telling her that. . .)

And as for Peaches . . . well, Peaches had slunk off somewhere too. I'd probably find him snoring on my desk in the den later, acting like his trek halfway across town had never happened.

"D'you think Rachel would like to hear me sing my song?" chattered Ellie, scuffing warm sand between her bare toes.

"No," said TJ bluntly.

"Yes," I said more sympathetically, shooting TJ a don't-wind-your-sister-up-she's-only-five-remember glare.

"Rachel is a very good singer so I'll have to do it *properly*," said Ellie earnestly, managing to either miss or ignore TJ's boyishly blunt "humour". "Maybe I could practise again in front of you – or that upside-down girl?"

"Magical thinking" . . . it's something tiny kids do. Mum told me about it after she read a book about child development, when Jamie had started freaking her out by babbling on about a "bad mouse" that lived in his wellies. It's just that really little kids get their worlds muddled up – they sometimes overlap the real stuff with stories they've heard and dreams they've had.

So Ellie's upside-down girl had to be part of her fantasy world, right? Only maybe she was getting a bit old for that.

And, er, actually . . . there *was* an upside-down girl.

She was hanging by the back of her knees over the blue railings on the prom, near Rachel's mum's shop. Her arms and blonde-ish hair were trailing in the sand, and her mouth was smiling. Oh, no – wait a minute – she was upside down, so really her mouth was in the miserable, down-turned position. (Obvious, really, *if* I was standing on my head.)

"It's *her* again – the cartwheeling girl!" whispered TJ.

"Her name's Megan and she's extra special nice," said Ellie, adjusting her deelyboppers so they were on straight. "She was crossing her eyes and trying to make me laugh when we were waiting to go on stage. And she was really good at being bendy."

"Yep, I guess she *was* good at being bendy!" said

TJ, glancing first at Ellie, then at me (with a grin), then at the upside-down girl.

I didn't manage a grin back because I was too busy trying to get the upside-down girl's attention. I know it wasn't my fault, and Kayleigh and her cronies were nothing to do with me, but I felt bad and had an urge to apologize for their boos and obnoxiousness.

"Um, hi. . ." I said pretty loudly.

But Bob had beaten me to it. Before the end of my "um", he'd bounded across and started licking Megan – who fell off her bat-perch as she wriggled and giggled, trying to get away from his doggy breath.

"Bob! *Heel!!*" yelled TJ, as Bob cheerfully ignored him and carried on his friendly licking campaign. "Sorry – he just gets a bit over-enthusiastic!"

"WHAT?" said Megan loudly, peeking over the top of Bob's general hairiness, and pulling a pair of tiny headphones out of her ears.

"Hey. . . What's going on?"

The new voice doing the asking sounded a bit wary. The new voice doing the asking belonged to Rachel.

"Hey, hi!" I said, smiling at her. "How did you get on this morning?"

Rachel threw a frown my way, which said "Not in front of this stranger!" and made me feel as thick as a solid red London brick.

"It was OK. . ." she answered blankly, staring hard at me and TJ, as if she was trying to fire a question straight into our brains; possibly about who exactly this girl was and why we were talking to her. (Rachel still needed her jaded edges of attitude – *bad* attitude – rubbed off. Still, the only thing she'd seen of this cartwheeling hit-and-runner had been her hurtling into me. She didn't have any idea about Megan being kind and funny to Ellie, or being unfairly booed after her turn at the talent show, or Peaches giving her his spook-cat seal of approval, just like he'd done for TJ and Rachel before. . .)

"God, *you're* the girl from yesterday! I am SOOOOO sorry!" gasped the girl called Megan, parting Bob's furry coat so she could see me better. "I was SOOOOOO embarrassed!"

"That's OK," I shrugged, feeling a slight twinge in my back that I hadn't noticed before I got slam-dunked by her.

"And omigod, *YOU*! You were BRILLIANT!" Megan suddenly said, from behind a licking dog.

The omigod thing; it was directed towards Rachel

this time. Rach opened her mouth and closed it again, not exactly sure *why* this girl trying to escape Bob's attentions thought she was brilliant.

"I was in the café on the prom on Sunday with my parents and my sister. I heard you singing that Madonna song on the karaoke machine – it was ACE! Much better than that girl who did it today at the talent show!"

"Actually, it was a Kylie track," Rachel corrected her, looking half-flattered at the compliment and half-confused about something. "Er . . . did someone sing 'Can't Get You Out of my Head' at the show today?"

The question was directed at me and TJ, but Ellie jumped right in with an answer.

"Yes – the not-nice girl who used to be your friend."

Rachel stared more intently at me and TJ.

"Kayleigh," I mumbled, aware of just how much it would hurt her. After all, two weeks ago, Kayleigh was one of Rachel's best mates in the world, along with Hazel and Brooke. Then just *one* week ago, they'd spectacularly proved they were no friends at all. And now with Kayleigh nicking Rachel's song . . . it must feel like yet *another* slap in the face.

"What?!" muttered Rachel, blinking hard. "But Kayleigh doesn't even *like* Kylie! She must have chosen that song just to have a go at me!"

God, I hoped this wasn't going to upset Rachel enough to bring on another of her seizures or something. . .

"I don't think it's so much *that*," I lied, thinking that might be *exactly* that. "I think it's 'cause Kayleigh saw you get tons of cheers and claps when you sang it at the café. She probably thinks a lot of the holidaymakers and everyone who heard you will be in the audience today, and—"

"What are you saying, Stella?" Rachel interrupted worriedly. "That people'll mistake *her* for *me*?"

Urgh, I hadn't meant it to come out like that at *all* . . . and now my brain was in such a tangle as I tried to think my way out of what I'd said that my mouth had gone blank.

"No way, Rach – no one could muddle *you* two up. I mean, the difference is that you were good, and Kayleigh was . . . *rotten*," TJ jumped in with a quick dollop of reassurance instead.

"*And* she had on a *bra*," said Ellie, wide-eyed at the horror of it.

"*And* she booed me. I never booed *her*," Megan added glumly.

Rachel looked like she might have been about to say more up until the point Megan spoke. Then it was as if she'd spotted the stranger in our midst all over again and decided to shut right up about *anything* personal.

"Anyway, Rach, there're two more heats for the talent show," TJ cheerfully chattered on. "We entered you for the one on Thursday!"

"You could sing *any* song and you'd be BRILLIANT!"

As she trotted out that compliment, Megan started fidgeting with the posh looking i-Pod clipped on to the top of her shorts.

"Don't know if you'd like *this* track. Haven't got a clue what it is exactly, but I LOVE it. Check it out!"

Megan offered her headphones to Rachel, who backed away as if Megan was holding out a jam jar of something radioactive.

"Here, give me a listen," said TJ, reaching out for the black headphones and sticking them in his ears instead. "Oh. . . Marilyn Manson?!"

I couldn't claim to be as much of a music know-all as TJ, but that name seemed familiar.

"Isn't he that really, really. . ."

I ground to a halt, wondering if I'd got it wrong

and would embarrass myself.

". . .scary goth singer that could easily be in a horror movie?" TJ finished for me, slipping off the earphones again.

Ah, so I was right. And no wonder he'd been surprised to hear Megan's choice of music – she looked more like a Girl Guide than a hard-bitten goth-rock fan.

"Oh, I got the i-Pod from my big sister. I don't know what songs are stored on there. . ."

Pretty generous sister, I thought to myself, wondering how much something that fancy cost.

"When I say I *got* it from my sister, I mean she lent it to me," said Megan, taking the headphones back and fidgeting with a flapping piece of red tape wound round the black plastic cable.

"Lucky you," shrugged Rachel, deciding to join in the conversation again. "My big brother wouldn't lend me his i-Pod or *any* of his stuff in a million years!"

"My sister Naomi lends me LOADS of stuff."

"Is she some kind of a saint?" I grinned at Megan.

"God, NO! I mean, she's pretty cool and everything, but she's no saint. She's just sort of *bribing* me, I guess. . ."

"Huh? Why's she bribing you?" I asked, intrigued.

I noticed that we'd all moved in a little closer, to hear more (well, except for Ellie and Bob, who didn't know what bribing *meant*).

"'Cause I'm her excuse. 'Cause the first day we got to Portbay Naomi got in with this crowd . . . she's fifteen and they're WAY older – about seventeen or something," Megan explained, drumming her fingers on the i-Pod as if she was still listening to Marilyn Manson. "Anyway, Naomi's been hanging out with them the whole of the holidays so far, but tells Mum and Dad she's with *me*."

"But why does she do that?" asked TJ.

"'Cause our mum and dad are totally cool about us mooching round the beach or the shops if we're together; it means they can go hiking for hours without worrying about us," said Megan.

"Hiking?" said Rachel, like that was the naffest thing she'd ever heard.

"Yeah, they love it, and they know me and Naomi – specially Naomi – can't be bothered tramping up and down hills and stuff."

"Must be pretty nice that they trust you so much," I said. "Even if you are, er, both sort of *lying* to them. . ."

"Yeah, but then they're kind of strict in other ways," shrugged Megan, brushing over my comment. "I mean, they'd FLIP if they knew Naomi was fooling around with older kids. Specially if they knew she was SNOGGING one of them. . ."

"She's got a *boyfriend*? Like a *secret* boyfriend?" asked Rachel, her dark almond eyes widening at this dollop of excellent gossip.

"Yeah . . . so every day she goes off to meet her new friends and him, when he's not working at his summer job."

"And what do *you* do?" I asked.

Megan stuck her lower lip out and glanced upwards, as if she was thinking hard for a suitable answer.

"Dunno. Just sort of MOOCH, I guess! Practise my cartwheels on the beach. See how long I can make an ice-cream last for!"

"Doesn't that get boring?" TJ asked, in his typically boyishly blunt way.

"Well, *yeah*, but then Naomi lends me excellent stuff like THIS, which helps pass the time a bit," said Megan, holding up the i-Pod. "And this is really cool, 'cause it's actually her boyfriend's and it's like, MEGA!"

"Yeah, it's pretty flash," TJ agreed, "but it still must be kind of dull, just wandering around town on your own."

"It's OK," Megan shrugged again. "But sometimes it's more like *annoying*, 'cause Naomi never meets me when she says she will, so we get back to the caravan later than we promised and my parents freak out at us BOTH!"

"Sounds like she's a pain in the—"

I'm sure TJ was going to come out with something ruder than just "neck", but we never heard it 'cause Rachel butted in.

"That i-Pod. . ." she muttered, a frown forcing her delicate eyebrows together as she stared hard at the flap of red tape wound around the black cable of the headphones. "It's *Si*'s! It's my brother's! I recognize that bit of tape! What are you doing with my brother's i-Pod?!"

Duh. . .

Maybe Rachel might be missing the obvious, but I couldn't blame her. After all, my friend Frankie started secretly dating the boy I had a *huge* crush on about five seconds after I left London, and I didn't manage to spot a single clue.

"'Si' as in *Simon*?!" Megan blurted out, ignoring Rachel's accusing tone. "Yeah – THAT'S his name!

He's got a pierced lip, right? And he always wears T-shirts with stuff like 'Death Metal Kitty' on them!"

"Oh, yeah! He wears that one a *lot*," said TJ, nodding in agreement.

For a second, Rachel looked muddled, the truth *still* not quite sinking into her pretty head.

"The boy Megan's sister is snogging. . ." I began to spell it out for her.

". . .it's your brother!" TJ jumped in.

"Um, does that mean you and you are related now?" Ellie asked, her deelyboppers swirling in confusion as she stared from a grinning Megan to a gobsmacked Rachel and back again.

From Megan's expression, you could see that she was pretty chuffed to be linked – however daftly – to someone like Rachel.

Rachel, on the other hand, looked faintly *faint* at the idea of being "related" to this cartwheeling oddball who couldn't manage a sentence without a least one word in shouty, over-enthusiastic capitals.

"COOL!" laughed Megan.

"*Weird*. . ." mumbled Rachel darkly.

Chapter 4

COOL! BRILLIANT! ACE!

Megan was mesmerized by the fake fairies.

And when someone's mesmerized (by fake fairies or whatever), it means they're usually too busy to notice if they're being gossiped about.

"That girl Megan – she's a bit . . . *much*," said TJ.

"That girl Megan" was currently staring at four framed photos hanging on one of the display stands dotted around the town hall foyer. Ellie was helpfully pointing to the various fake fairies in the pictures and then doing twirls in her own fairy costume (and noisy tap shoes).

It had been a couple of hours since the talent show, and we were in the town hall, where loads of Gala Week events were happening, including performances of *The Roar of the Rainforest* – written, directed by and starring TJ and Ellie's mum, as we could see from the poster on the wall. But this afternoon we were here in the foyer of the town hall to check out the art exhibition that Rachel's mum had organized. And there, amongst the still lives of mouldy fruit and wonky watercolours of triangles that were meant to be yachts, were the fairies, flitting around a wild tangle of dark ivy, old roses and droopily tall foxgloves.

The fairies were – fanfare, please – all my own work. I'd painted them, cut them out, taped them on to thin green garden canes and snapped them with Mum's camera. Of course, I couldn't have done the Fake Fairy Photo Project without TJ's art direction. Um . . . when I say *art direction*, I mean that TJ placed all the fairies artistically before I took the photos. (OK, so he *rammed* the garden canes into the ground here and there. . .)

"She's not just a bit much, she's a bit mad!" Rachel muttered under her breath, staring daggers into Megan's back.

"I don't think she's *mad*, exactly!" I said in Megan's defence, wishing Rachel wouldn't be so harsh. "She's just a bit talkative, and bouncy, and. . ."

". . .and *mad*, Stella!" TJ laughed. "In the last two hours she's never shut up, and she's never stood still for more than five seconds!"

OK, so Megan *was* kind of full-on – she'd done ninety percent of the yakking while we'd got ourselves hotdogs for lunch and wandered round Portbay, noseying at the street performers and general Gala Week gubbins. And she's one of these people who can't talk without their arms acting out every sentence and comment. Then in the ten percent of the time that she'd let me or TJ or Rachel or Ellie get a word in edgeways, she constantly drummed her fingers on her legs or frantically clicked her fingers. (You know how dogs can hear high frequencies and cats can stare at walls seeing stuff humans can't? Well, maybe Megan was tuned into some frantic hip-hop beat that only *she* could hear. . .)

"Yes, but Megan's been on her own most of her holiday so far," I reminded my not-too-charitable friends. "Maybe she's just a bit hyper 'cause she's got people to hang out with at last."

"Remind me, Stella; why are *we* the people she happens to be hanging out with?" Rachel mumbled, sympathy not exactly oozing out of every pore.

"You're just hacked off 'cause your brother's dating her sister and you didn't know about it," TJ teased Rachel. (The thing with Kayleigh and the Kylie song was probably still niggling at her too.)

"I am *not* hacked off about that!" Rachel protested, though I didn't think me and TJ completely believed her. "As if Si would ever tell me anything anyway. Still, *now* I get why he was skiving off work so many days last week. . ."

"Yeah, yeah," said TJ, breezily ignoring Rachel's ratty tone. "Anyway, y'see the way Megan's staring at the fairy pictures, trying to think of something to say about them? I bet you she comes out with 'COOL!' any second now. . ."

Famous people might have catchphrases, but in the short time we'd known her, it dawned on us that mad old Megan had catch-*words*. And it seemed that everything in Megan's World was either COOL! or BRILLIANT! or ACE!

You want examples? Well. . .

COOL! stuff according to Megan: her sister Naomi; the colour purple; *The Princess Diaries*; cheesecake; Alton Towers Theme Park; gymnastics; dogs; the movie *Shrek 2* (WAY! cooler than the first *Shrek* movie, apparently); writing your name in the dust on cars; and the extreme skill of the crystal ball loop-de-looper guy on the prom.

BRILLIANT! stuff according to Megan: riding bikes downhill fast; the smell of petrol (weird); the word "weird"; MTV; my curly-swirly honey-coloured hair (thanks for the compliment); old people paddling in the sea; the fact that *technically* starfish don't have fronts and backs; and Mr and Mrs Mystic Marzipan's amazingly life-like balloon anteater that we'd just seen being blown and bent into existence.

ACE! stuff according to Megan: Monster Munch crisps; holidays in caravans; finding stupid shapes in constellations of stars; how snails can unfurl their horns; typing your own name into Google and seeing what comes up; and Bob nearly weeing on the rubbish human statue (who was still rubbish, even *without* the psycho seagull swirling ominously overhead).

"Nah, it's not going to be 'COOL!'. I bet you a packet of crisps she says 'BRILLIANT!'" I said to TJ.

"So what does that leave me with? Oh, yeah – 'ACE!'" Rachel chipped in, breaking into a smile at last.

"Y'know something, Megan? There was a nice photo of Bob's nose sniffing at the camera, but they didn't put that in the exer-bition," we suddenly heard Ellie trill loudly, as she spun herself around, floaty dress and feather boa spiralling out.

"Yeah?" said Megan, nodding down at Ellie

before she swivelled round to face us. "Hey, guys – these are just really, really. . ."

Me, TJ and Rachel waited, breath caught in the back of our throats, to see who'd win the bet.

". . .totally AWESOME!" Megan finished her sentence, throwing in a whole new LOUD adjective we hadn't heard her say before. "They look so REAL! Where did you take them?"

"In the overgrown garden at Joseph's house," I said, stepping closer to Megan, Ellie and my artwork. "If you're staying at the caravan park, you can probably see it – it's in Sugar Bay, on the opposite side of the headland from Portbay."

"God, yeah! COURSE I can see it out of the caravan – it's that old, falling-down wreck, right?"

I might have had a tug of sympathy for Megan, and she might have given me a nice compliment about my hair earlier on, but I couldn't help getting this little wriggle of annoyance at what she'd just said. Maybe it was kind of nuts to feel protective about a house, but I did, specially after unearthing all the bits of history around it that I had.

"It's maybe a wreck *now*," I muttered and shrugged, "but it was a pretty fancy place once. And I don't suppose the people who used to live there would exactly *love* the view of some scuzzy old caravans out of their windows, if they were alive to see them."

"But caravans are FUN!" said Megan brightly, as if she hadn't picked up on how bugged I was just there. "They're like doll's houses in a way – everything's in miniature!"

"Could I maybe see your little house?" Ellie asked sweetly, looking up wide-eyed at Megan.

"Yeah! Course you can! You could ALL come, if you fancy. Maybe tomorrow morn—"

A terrible, *terrible* noise suddenly started up somewhere in the square outside the town hall. From all the thumping, screeching and honking going on, if someone told me a herd of sadistic elephants were trampling a flock of geese, I'd have believed them.

Still, geese-torturing elephants don't tend to stomp in *time* with one another. . .

"Jeez, not *that* lot!" TJ moaned loudly, shaking his head wearily.

"What? Who are they?" I asked, peeking out and seeing a muddle of wine and gold uniforms and the glint of brass.

"The Portbay Youth Orchestra," Rachel yelled above the racket, rolling her eyes. "It's a running joke in town that they're so terrible that no one

60

ever knows what tunes they're trying to play!"

I strained for a second, thinking it might be "Mull of Kintyre", or then again, the National Anthem, or maybe even the theme to *Star Trek*. Whatever it was, it didn't exactly fit the description of "music". And whatever it was, it was now being accompanied by a yowling howling, courtesy of Bob, who was parked outside by a railing.

"Hey, *told* you she was mad!" said TJ, nudging me in the arm.

I glanced over in Megan's direction in time to see her swooping Ellie around in a looky-likey old-time waltz move. She'd stuck a snooty look on her face, while Ellie giggled and tip-tapped on the marble flagstones as she struggled to keep up.

"Well, if Megan's mad, then what's Ellie?" I asked, grinning as I watched them joke-dance to the honking and screeching.

"Five years old, so *she* gets away with it!" said TJ, grinning broadly.

We weren't the only ones grinning. Plenty of people who'd been gawping at the mouldy fruit and triangular yacht pictures were finding it far more entertaining to watch the ditzy teenager whirl the shrieking little kid around the hall.

Except for Rachel, of course, with her what-*do*-you-look-like scowl.

"Is she a friend of yours?" said a cheery woman's voice, as an arm slipped around my shoulders, and Rachel's too.

Mrs Riley – Rachel's mum – was gazing at the waltzers. She'd already seen Ellie (and Bob) tagging along with me and TJ, so she could only be talking about Megan.

"Yes!"

"No!"

"Someone should put a hat down beside them," Mrs Riley laughed, oblivious to the fact that me and Rachel had answered her question with complete opposites. "Those girls are better than a lot of the street performers – they could make a fortune!"

"Why are you here?" Rachel challenged her mum all of a sudden.

Y'know, over the last week or so, I'd seen a really great side to Rachel (she got her mum interested in my fairy photos, after all), but those glimpses of the old, spoilt, intolerant Rachel still bugged me. Like the way she snapped at her mum, for one thing. And the way she wouldn't give Megan a chance. . . Was it 'cause Megan's sister was dating Si? Or was it 'cause Megan was the kind of uncool, unhip, ditzy girl that Rachel wouldn't have tolerated for a *micro*-second when she hung out with her snobby little clique of Kayleigh and co?

I knew Rachel had had a really rubbish time lately with the shock of her epilepsy and all the hospital tests and stuff, and it couldn't have been any fun finding out about Kayleigh's turn at the talent show today, but none of it was an excuse for behaving badly. . .

"Just popped by to see how the exhibition was going," Mrs Riley said brightly, brushing aside Rachel's snippiness. "But I'm heading home in a minute. Are you coming?"

With her scowl still fixed on Megan, Rachel gave a vague shrug and went to follow her mum. And she wasn't the only one to suddenly desert me.

"Urgh – is that the time?" TJ suddenly said, checking his watch. "I've got to get Ellie to her ballet class. . ."

Two minutes later – with both my friends (and Ellie) gone – I found myself on the stairs of the town hall with a girl I didn't know very well, listening to a brass band play a song I couldn't recognize at all.

"Well, better get home, I guess," I said to Megan, feeling a flutter of familiar shyness now that I was on my own with her.

"Oh, right. . ." Megan nodded, looking a little lost all of a sudden.

It was as if someone had turned down her volume and bounce controls from ten to one.

"So, what are you up to, then?" I asked tentatively.

"I guess I'll just . . . wander around a bit more. I'm not meeting up with Naomi for another couple of hours."

Instantly, I was in a quandary (that's a muddle, by the way, and not some kind of cave, like I used to think when I first heard the word as a kid). Should I be a really nice person and invite Megan back to my place? Or would it be a bit awkward, seeing as I didn't know her that well, and felt stupidly shy now that TJ and Rachel had gone?

Being really nice, or being stupidly shy. . .

Really nice, or stupidly shy. . .

It wasn't a difficult choice; in fact it came really naturally to someone like me.

"Er . . . well, bye then!" I smiled nervously, waving as I edged away from Megan, feeling like a (stupidly shy) meanie with every step I took.

"Bye!" Megan waved back, blinking her bright eyes my way and looking more of a little girl than Ellie all of a sudden.

I turned and hurried off, already imagining her sitting all alone on a bench on the prom at six o'clock – when everyone else had gone home for tea – with only a bag of chips and a hungry psycho seagull for company. . .

"Hey, Stella!"

Uh-oh – Megan wasn't going to ask if she could come back to mine, was she? Maybe I was being a meanie but that would be being *too* pushy.

"Yeah?" I said, turning to talk, but still walking backwards.

"The Sneezy Lemony!" Megan suddenly yelled above a particularly flat bit of honking from the trombone players.

"What?" I yelled back, wondering what she was on about.

"That's the name of our caravan! If you and TJ and Rach wanna come, I'll be there all tomorrow morning!"

"Yeah, maybe!" I said, feeling all in a quandary again. And confused. Who'd name a caravan the Sneezy Lemony?

But back to my quandary. Megan and Rachel,

Rachel and Megan. . . I couldn't see *how* the two of them were going to get along. I'd only known Megan for a few hours and she'd be leaving on Saturday, so was it worth hanging out with her and hacking off Rachel? But if Rachel was going to act more of a meanie than *I'd* been just now, wasn't that going to bug me pretty badly too?

Wow, this friendship thing was complicated. Three weeks ago, I'd arrived in Portbay and could count my mates here on no fingers. Now I had a handful and didn't know to handle them at *all*.

I needed to talk this over with someone. For a second I thought about phoning Frankie or one of my other old friends, but then I decided that old friends aren't necessarily the best people to give advice about *new* friends (they probably just think "Hmm . . . he/she doesn't sound *nearly* as good a mate as *I* was!").

Actually, the best type of person to give advice on friends might just be a *non*-friend. . .

Chapter 5

A very good non-friend of mine

The first non-friend I thought I could talk to was Mum. But when I got back home, Jake was in the middle of a tantrum so bad that his face was turning purple, and Mum was kind of preoccupied with trying to get him to stop screaming long enough to *breathe*.

The second non-friend I thought I'd try talking to was Dad, but he was busy showing a building inspector from the council around the house and smiling nervously while the inspector frowned at the wall Dad had just knocked down. (Dad had his fingers crossed behind his back again, I noticed.)

So I'd decided to go to my room and phone a very good non-friend of mine.

"The thing is, Auntie V, I know TJ isn't exactly *mad* on Megan, but he wasn't *mean* about her, the way Rachel was. And now Megan's invited me to the caravan tomorrow, but I just don't know if I should go. 'Cause if I go, and get the others along too, will Rachel just act all horrible to Megan? Or will she *refuse* to come and then go weird on me and TJ?"

"Don't fret so much, Stella my little star," said Auntie V in her elegant purr of a voice. It was easy to picture her in my head, sitting in her arty London office in her expensive designer clothes, a million miles away (if you see what I mean) from our messy muddle of a house by the sea.

"But I can't help it!" I frowned.

Didn't Auntie V know me at *all* after thirteen years? Didn't she know I was very good at fretting? Didn't she know it's the perfect hobby for people like me, who suffer from a serious case of shyness? (Well, I was getting better at being confident, but a girl can't give up all her hobbies just like *that*, now can she?)

"Don't take it the wrong way, sweetheart," Auntie V drawled down the phone. "I just think you're maybe overlooking something with your friend Rachel."

"Like what?" I asked, putting my head and the phone under my duvet in the hope that it might block out the sound of Jake's screaming heeby-jeebies.

"Maybe Rachel's acting out of sorts today because

for the last week or so, you've been looking after *her*, but then today, you've been more interested in this new girl's feelings. Maybe Rachel's just a tiny bit hurt that you're not so interested in what's going on with her. I'm not making excuses for her, I'm just trying to think of a reason why she could be acting so cool towards. . ."

BLAM!

Right in the middle of what Auntie V was saying, it dawned on me – with a big old thunk of the heart – that thanks to hanging out with Megan all afternoon, I hadn't got round to asking Rachel how she'd got on at the doctor's.

So maybe that is *why she seemed to resent Megan so much!* I thought, immediately tossing the duvet aside and sitting up straight on the bed. As soon as it didn't come across as being rude, I'd have to get off the phone to Auntie V and call Rachel straight away to put that right.

"Oh, Stella, darling, I'm sorry but a taxi's just arrived to take me to the rehearsal of a play that one of my clients is in. I've got to go, I'm afraid," muttered Auntie V, as a horn parped in the background.

"That's OK," I told her, feeling relieved that I didn't have to make any excuses to finish our conversation.

"Oh, and one last thing, Stella. . ."

"Uh-huh?"

"Whichever one of your brothers is making that terrible racket . . . can you go and see if there's somewhere on him you can take the batteries out?"

Ah, if *only*. . .

Ten minutes and a lot of chatting later, I was pretty sure that Rachel just generally didn't like Megan – i.e. it had nothing at all to do with me forgetting to ask about her doctor's appointment.

Oh, dear. . .

"*Please* say we don't have to go!" she pleaded with me.

"Well, you don't have to come," I said, lying back on my bed with the mighty weight of a purring Peaches on my chest. "But I just thought it could be kind of fun. And we might meet Megan's sister Naomi. Don't you want to have a nosey at the girl your brother's going out with?"

By the way, Rachel had got on OK at the doctor's. He hadn't given her a hard time for missing out a chunk of info that might be important, and said they wouldn't start her on any drugs until the results of all her tests were in and they'd monitored her for a few weeks, to see if she had any more seizures or not. In the meantime, she just had to promise to eat proper meals and get enough sleep, 'cause that could make a real difference to her health.

Once we'd talked through the doctor stuff, I'd wondered if I should bring up the subject of the invite to Megan's caravan in the morning, or just forget about it and not go.

It was quandary time again. But as my brain flipped between mentioning Megan's invite or not, Peaches stood upright and leant over me, looming his mammoth face into mine. Maybe he was trying to tell me it was tea-time, or maybe it was something (spookily) else altogether.

And *that*'s when I blurted out about visiting Megan (and the weirdly named Sneezy Lemony), and *that*'s when Rachel started pleading with me not to go. But since Peaches had began a chest-vibrating purrathon, I figured I'd done the right thing.

"I mean, I wouldn't *mind* checking out who Si's snogging," Rachel said now. "But not if I have to hang out with Megan!"

"What have you got against her?"

"She's just . . . annoying and *silly*!"

"Silly's all right!" I laughed, picturing Megan handstanding her way around the stage this morning, and waltzing Ellie round the art exhibition.

"Grow up, Stella!" Rachel snorted, a horrible slant of sarkiness in her voice.

Bubbles of irritation and hurt rippled through my chest. No one had ever talked to me like that! I mean, yeah, so Frankie and Neisha back in London could sometimes be a bit mouthy and tease me, but they'd only be fooling around, never being cruel.

"Whatever. . ." I said in a clipped, get-off-my-case voice, and slammed my finger on the end-call key.

Tears of not-fairness prickled at my eyes.

"Why's Rachel got to be like that?" I asked Peaches, whose nose was practically resting on my chin. "I've always been nice to *her*. God, I even helped save her from *drowning*!"

"Prrrrrrrr. . ." purred Peaches, as my head filled with thoughts of Rachel's first seizure, when she fell into the pool at the lido and sank unconscious to the bottom. Maybe the lifeguard would have got her out in time if me and TJ hadn't been there, but then again, maybe he wouldn't have. And what kind of thanks did I get? Rachel slipping into her bad, old Kayleigh and co ways and sniping at me.

"And what kind of answer is 'prrrrrrr'?" I demanded, lifting my head just enough to look into Peaches' eyes, and at the same time give myself a very attractive double chin. "Anyway, *you're* the one who persuaded me she was OK!"

At that, Peaches gave a wide, tuna-scented yawn and bounded off me, trotting towards my open bedroom window and leaving me with my nicely tangled thoughts.

"Thanks!" I called after him, wondering how I could get the number of a local psychiatric clinic that specialized in Hallucinating That Your Cat Can Communicate With You.

Hopping up on to the window sill, Peaches completely ignored me – but glanced back around as soon as my mobile began ringing.

"I'm not answering it," I told Peaches, immediately recognizing Rachel's number on the neon green display.

For the whole of the eight rings, Peaches stared at me with his neon green eyes, like he was willing me to put my pride aside and see what Rachel had to say.

But sometimes us shy girls can be quite stubborn. So, ignoring the phone and Peaches, I picked up a magazine lying by my bedside.

It wasn't till a few minutes and a lot of fuming later that I realized the magazine was upside down – and Peaches was still on the window sill staring at me.

"What?" I asked, just as the "bleep!" of an incoming text made me jump.

Maybe it would be Frankie, or Neisha or one of the girls, sending me a *hi-how-u-doing?* message back . . . but no – it was from Rachel.

SOZ!! What time 4 Megan's 2moz? Rach x

Well, it wasn't what you'd call a full apology, but I guess I'd accept a "SOZ", specially since it was in capitals.

Should I let her off with that? I asked myself, staring at the text.

"Prrrrp!" prrrped Peaches, before leaping down from the ledge on to the kitchen roof, and off to wherever his excessive wanderings would take him.

Hmm, you *could* say that he was reading my thoughts and that "prrrrp!" was his reply, or you *could* say that I should grab the Yellow Pages and try to find a number for that psychiatric clinic *now* . . .

Chapter 6

Shivers of the spine-swivelling kind

"So how about it?" said TJ, spreading the four tickets out on the plastic-topped table in the caravan. The caravan that was called the Sea Anemone. Not the Sneezy Lemony. (Must have sand in my ears. . .)

"Tonight? Yeah, whatever. Anything to get away from my nagging mum," Rachel answered TJ, her face scrunched up in a grimace.

(Note: when Rachel's face is scrunched up in a grimace, she still looks gorgeous in that Siamese cat way of hers. When *I* scrunch my face up in a grimace, I probably look like someone has rearranged my face and put it back in slightly the wrong order.)

TJ was trying to rustle up more takers for this evening's performance of *The Roar of the Rainforest*. I'd already said yes, of course, and now it seemed like Rachel was grudgingly up for it too. Megan, meanwhile, was nervously fidgeting with the blind cord of the caravan window, as if TJ's invitation couldn't be meant for her too.

"Megan?"

At TJ's mention of her name, Megan flushed pink with a severe case of chuffed-ness, and grinned as wide as wide can be. Then in a flash, her grin faded.

"Can't do it – got to cover for Naomi again, haven't I? She's already figured out a story and told Mum and Dad. And she's said to them we'll be back here by eight."

"No worries." TJ shrugged casually, pocketing the tickets – not noticing how disappointed Megan looked.

But then we all suddenly noticed the horrified expression on Rachel's face. . .

"*Eeeeeyewww!* Has Bob been eating cat food again?"

"No – he just rolled in a pond on the way here," TJ explained to Rachel.

"What kind of pond – one that something *died* in?"

"It *was* kind of stagnant, I guess," TJ admitted.

"There was flies flying above it," said Ellie seriously, as she carried on glancing around the caravan, fascination glinting in her baby blue eyes.

"Don't worry – I'll open another window. . ."

As Megan spoke, she knelt on one of the banquettes that lined three sides of the far end of the caravan, and wrestled with a window latch.

Bob, oblivious to the fuss he was causing, panted happily on the pale woolly rug on the floor.

"I've got a better idea," said TJ, standing up and padding over to the door. "Bob! Where's your ball? Where's the ball? Is it out here?"

TJ did an excellent job of throwing an imaginary tennis ball. Well, it was excellent enough to fool Bob, who went clattering out of the caravan door – which was then firmly closed behind him.

"Poor Bob!" I couldn't help saying.

"He'll be fine," TJ said, padding back to join us. "He'll keep busy trying to find it for a while, then he'll find a moth or a speck of dust to chase instead."

"Your house isn't as little as I thought it would be."

That was Ellie, a flicker of disappointment now visible on her face. Maybe she'd hoped to find mouse-sized bunk-beds and thimbles for cups.

"Yeah, but it's pretty nice though, isn't it, Ellie?"

I thought I owed Megan that much – from outside, the Sea Anemone was still a big, ugly hulk of metal, but inside it was kind of cute, with everything neatly tucked away, no space wasted, and a modern, seasidey colour scheme of bleached wood and sand that even my design-snob Auntie V might approve of.

"I like watching the gulls out of the window from my top bunk in the morning," Megan smiled. "The view from my bedroom at home is just of another block of flats."

We hadn't seen Megan's bedroom yet – she shared it with Naomi, and Naomi was still sleeping, even though it was nearly half-eleven. We'd seen Megan's mum and dad's room (just big enough to swing a kitten round in), though we hadn't seen *them*, since they were out hiking to some Iron Age dwelling or whatever in a faraway field.

"See Joseph's house down there?" I said, pointing to the old mansion down in the otherwise empty cove of Sugar Bay. "The old lady who grew up there, she was called Elize Grainger, and she had this plan to build a centre up here for underprivileged kids from the city. It never happened though, which is a bit of a shame. . ."

"But it *did* happen, in a way!" Megan grinned.

Um . . . hadn't Megan heard what I said just now? Elize – who'd become a bit of a heroine of mine since I'd found out so much about her, including the fact that she'd spent her retirement in the cottage we now lived in – had never seen her dream come true. She'd never managed to sell Joseph's house and raise the money for her centre, and had to leave it to fall to rack and ruin (whatever "rack" was).

"Well, I'm not exactly *underprivileged*, but my parents don't have that much money!" Megan pointed out. "They can't afford to take me and Naomi abroad, or stay in some fancy hotel somewhere. So we come to different caravan parks every year and have a BRILLIANT! time. Well, *usually* we have a brilliant time, but this year's been a bit different 'cause of Naomi going off with her new friends and—"

"Poo! Did something *die* in here?!"

A vision appeared from the closed doorway that we knew led to Megan and Naomi's room. The vision was dressed in a lilac vest top and flowery, hip-hugging pyjama bottoms, with a couple of entwined leather bracelets round one wrist. The vision had messy, blonde, bed-heady hair, which she was currently scratching her hand through. The vision looked sleepy and had the remnants of last night's eye make-up fudged and smudged around her eyes, but – like Rachel with the grimace – still looked completely, amazingly, drop-dead gorgeous.

I felt like leaning over and pushing TJ's chin up for him so his mouth would close. Any second now, his tongue might loll out, like Bob's did at the sight of a tin of cat food.

"Hi, Naomi!" said Megan, her face lighting up in the presence of her sister. "It was just TJ's dog, but I've opened the windows so it should be fine in a sec! Anyway, these are my friends: this is Stella, that's TJ and this is Rachel!"

"Yeah, right. Um, hi. . ." muttered Naomi distractedly, grabbing herself a glass and rifling around for juice in the fridge that was disguised as a narrow cupboard. "Listen, change of plan tonight, Megan. Me and Si and his mates are going to Westbay later this afternoon, to catch a movie, and then we're going for a pizza. I won't be back in Portbay till about nine, so just meet you at the usual bench round about then?"

I sneaked a quick look at Rachel, to see what she made of both Naomi and the mention of her brother. I think it's fair to say the expression on her face read "gobsmacked". The ruling teen queen of gorgeousness had just met her (two years older) match, and her match just happened to be dating her brother.

"But that's *really* late . . . we won't get back here till half-nine – IF you're on time! Mum and Dad'll have a FIT!" squeaked Megan, looking worried.

"Nah – they'll be OK." Naomi yawned. "I'll think of an excuse. I'll say you're doing something with your mates, and you're dragging me along."

"My mum's got a theatre show on tonight – me and Stella and Rachel are all going," TJ offered.

"Where? And when it's on till?" asked Naomi, narrowing her eyes at TJ and making him blush to the roots of his floppy brown hair.

"Town hall. Till half-nine," TJ mumbled, turning all bashful in Naomi's older, confident presence.

"Perfect – Mum and Dad'll buy that," murmured Naomi, taking a slug of her juice. "I'll tell 'em when they get back from their hike to wherever. . ."

Megan bit her lip, as if she was a) worried about the lie her sister was about to spin, and b) worried about saying no to her big sister. Or maybe she was just c) worried about how to fill so many empty hours. . .

TJ must've thought it was a case of c).

"Hey, so I guess that means you *can* come to the show tonight now – yeah, Megan?"

"Um, yeah . . . OK, then," Megan smiled at TJ, before turning her attention back to her big sister. "Naomi, I just thought of something. . . D'you remember I told you about Rachel last night? How she's Simon's sister?"

That seemed to penetrate Naomi's sleepy fug. Her cutely scruffy head of hair emerged from behind the door and she eyed us all up, finally settling her gaze on Rachel.

"Me and Simon – this is a secret, right? You're not going to blab, OK?"

"Uh. . ." mumbled Rachel, flummoxed in the face of such a specific order. "Fine. Whatever."

"Hey! Anyone fancy going down to check out that old house? That would be FUN, right!" Megan blurted out, smiling but looking kind of anxious around the edges. Was she embarrassed 'cause of Naomi suddenly giving Rachel a hard time?

"Sounds great – let's go!" I said enthusiastically, suddenly keen to get out of this small, bad-vibey, smelly-dog-scented space and into the fresh, sea-breezy air of Sugar Bay. . .

*

"It's ACE! that Dad forgot to take this with him today!"

"Give me a go – how d'you switch it on?" asked TJ, taking the metal detector from Megan.

"There. . . And then you have to sweep it slowly along the beach from side to si—"

"You're never going to find anything with *that* glorified mop!" Rachel interrupted, before ambling after Ellie, who was picking tiny flowers that were somehow growing between the sea-smoothed pebbles.

"Oh, yeah? Well, listen to the bleeping this thing's doing," TJ shouted over his shoulder. "It's definitely on to *something*!"

Y'know, so far this morning, Rachel had been on her best behaviour, trying to prove herself after yesterday's snippiness. But it was like she'd got bored with that game now and was reverting back to thoughtless sniping. When we'd wandered around inside Joseph's house a few minutes ago – showing Megan the tatty-edged grand rooms that would be disappearing when the place was demolished – Rachel had snorted out loud when Megan called the vast crystal chandelier a "*huuuuumongously* BIG lamp".

"Look, I'm sorry about Rachel. I don't think she

means it how it sounds," I found myself apologizing to Megan, now that Rachel was out of earshot.

TJ was out of earshot too, happily sweeping his way along the sands with Bob bouncing round the metal detector trying to figure out what kind of weird animal it was.

I hadn't wanted TJ to catch on to what I'd just said; out of the two of us, he was the one who was pretty wary of being friends with Rachel in the first place. And I didn't want him to go back to thinking badly of her – even if *I* was starting to. . .

"It's OK, I'm used to it," said Megan, shrugging her shoulders and shuffling her trainers noisily through the stones. "Rachel reminds me of Naomi, the way she talks. Maybe *all* pretty girls talk that way! Then again, *you* don't. . ."

For a second there, I'd been suddenly angry at the idea of "pretty" girls getting away with rude behaviour and was determined – even though I was rubbish at being bolshy – not to let Rachel get away with it again, whether she was talking to me, Megan or whoever. Then Megan went and threw a compliment my way – as casually as Rachel let rip sarky comments – and I was floored, my cheeks burning pink and any words just traffic-jammed in my mouth.

"Hey, in one of the leaflets in the caravan, it says there were pirates and smugglers round here!" said Megan, thankfully changing the subject. "Is that true?"

"Yeah – there's stuff about them in Portbay Museum."

(My stupid mind flipped from images of display cases with old coins in, to the only pirate I'd ever seen close up – the automated one that "yo-ho-ho!"d outside Portbay's miniature golf course. . .)

"This looks like the sort of cove they'd drop off treasure in, doesn't it?" grinned Megan, speeding up so that we could monitor TJ's progress with the metal detector. "Maybe we'll find enough buried treasure to pay to save that fancy big chandelier thing before the bulldozers move in!"

"Nice idea," I grinned. "TJ's on the trail of something, that's for sure. Though I bet it's more likely to be a whole bunch of old Coke cans instead of a casket of priceless Spanish doubloons!"

"I dunno what a doubloon is," Megan cheerfully admitted, "but I *do* know what the metal detector's detecting!"

"How come?" I asked, feeling a shiver up my spine and down again.

That had happened quite a few times since I'd moved to this weirdy little town. It had happened when Peaches was freaking me out with his general spook-catness. It happened a couple of times when I'd been exploring inside Joseph's house – like only last week, when Rachel had one of her strange, shaky episodes. I don't mean one of the seizures, but these bizarre kind of telepathic moments that'd been happening off and on *since* her first seizure. That time last week, she'd said that she could make out children playing hide and seek behind long-gone velvet drapes in the ballroom. . .

Was Megan tuned into the spooky side too?

"It's Bob's collar," she grinned my way.

"What?"

"Bob's collar! As soon as TJ switched the machine on, it picked up on the buckle and name tag on the collar! That's what TJ's following, and Bob just keeps chasing around the detector, so they could be there for hours!"

"Should we tell him?" I said from behind my hand, so TJ couldn't see me sniggering if he turned round.

"Why? It's funny!" Megan beamed at me.

So Megan might not be psychic, but she obviously wasn't just a mad, loud, annoying, cartwheeling airhead, or whatever else TJ and Rachel had her down as. She also had a (really) wicked sense of humour.

If only Rachel would give her a chance. But what would it take for Rachel to do that?

"TJ! Stella! Something's wrong!!" Ellie suddenly shrilled.

TJ cut the machine and turned round at the same time as me and Megan did.

Ellie was standing upright, fairy-sized bouquet in her fingers, staring up at an ashen-faced and stock-still Rachel, who in turn was staring straight down at a rippled section of damp sand.

In moments of panic, the stupidest things can jump into your mind, and all I could think of for a nano-second was that Rachel would make a much better human statue than the twitchy, blinking bloke down at the prom. . .

But then Megan – of all people – broke the (stupid) spell.

"Rachel's having a seizure again, isn't she?" she said all alarmed, as she began running towards her.

"No – it's not one of her seizures . . . it's this other thing that happens to her sometimes," I called out, running after her.

"It's like a funny turn," said TJ, arriving at Rachel first and resting his arm protectively around her waist, just in case she started to wobble. "What is it, Rach? What do you see?"

"I . . . I don't know," muttered Rachel, her gaze still cast down, and looking as confused as she had before when this had happened to her. "Something's under the sand. . . Maybe you need the detector thing."

TJ didn't need to be told twice. He zoomed back to the detector, which Bob was guarding, and quickly flicked it on.

"Ellie, grab Bob and stand back, honey," I told her, remembering that Bob (and his collar) needed to be out of the equation for anything to happen.

Bleeeeep! *Bleeeep!* *Burrrrr-LEEEEEEEEEEEPPP!*

With a few quick swings, the detector went mad, right around the spot Rachel was focused on.

"Did someone bring a spade?" asked TJ dejectedly, knowing the answer was no. "OK – don't worry. Bob! Here, boy! Dig! There's a good boy! That's right, just like I'm doing, dig!"

TJ had only scooped the slightest handful of sand for Bob to get the message, break free from Ellie and get to work.

The mound of sand grew higher and higher and his furry paws dug deeper and deeper, with all of us scanning the damp, golden mass for anything that wasn't a shell, a pebble or a wriggling, unidentified sand-bug.

"I just saw something!" Ellie squealed. "Look!"

Her small fingers burrowed around . . . and pulled out a chain, dull with age and long-burial, but still shimmering twinkles of the gold it must be made of.

"It's got one of those . . . what do girls call 'em?" asked TJ, taking the chain gently from Ellie.

"A locket!" I murmured, lifting the oval shape in my fingers and rubbing enough sand off to see swirls of engraving and an ornate letter in the middle.

"What is that? An H?" Megan frowned at it.

"No," I said softly, my heart bada-binging in my chest. "It's an E!"

Megan was still frowning. And why shouldn't she be? What did E mean to her? It could stand for Ellen or Elizabeth or Erica or a hundred other names, but the fact that we'd found it here, so close to Joseph's house, and the fact that Rachel had found it like she had . . . for me that meant only one thing.

"I think it's E for Elize," I told her, sensing the shivers swivelling up and down my spine for the second time in five minutes.

"Wait a minute!" Rachel suddenly said, raising her head and looking like her normal self again. "How did *you* know I'd had a seizure before?"

Her gaze was firmly on Megan. And then I found myself gazing at Megan too. How *did* she know about Rachel's seizures? None of *us* had mentioned them to her. . .

"You know I said I saw you singing the Madonna song at the café on Sunday?" she ventured, looking awkward.

"It was a *Kylie* song," Rachel corrected her for the second time.

"Well, that wasn't the first time I saw you do it. I was watching you from outside when you sang it before –"

Oh, yeah – there were crowds on the pavement, I remembered. Holidaymakers all gawping at the girl with the great voice, little guessing she was about to collapse. . .

"– that was the time you got taken ill," Megan continued warily, like she was worried she'd upset Rachel. "Anyway, my mum was the first to help you before the ambulance turned up – she's a nurse."

I'd wondered what it would take for Rachel to give Megan a chance, and I think that moment had just arrived. Rachel blinked at Megan, taking in the coincidence, and the kindness Megan had shown for not blurting that out yesterday when she first met us, and maybe stirring up bad memories for Rachel.

For the rest of this week, the four of us (well, four and two halves, if you count Ellie and Bob) might have a pretty interesting time now. Maybe we could hunt around here some more, and see what the metal detector – and Rachel – could pick up.

Meanwhile, as the four of us and Ellie stared at each other – our minds whirling with what the last few minutes had revealed to us – Bob happily dug and dug and dug, merrily on his way to Australia. . .

Chapter 7

A familiar face
(er, from a century or so ago)

Peaches blinked at me, looking more and more infuriatingly calm the more and more I struggled.

"It won't blimmin' *open*!" I finally growled, my nails chipped from trying – and failing – to get the locket to show me its secrets.

Me and the others had all left Sugar Bay and the strange morning well behind, promising to meet up later in the afternoon again. (Not to mention going out together to TJ's mum's show in the evening – hey, our schedule was pretty busy. . .)

In the meantime, I'd promised Mum I'd help her take Jake and Jamie shoe shopping this afternoon (it was easier with two, although a lasso would've been handy); Rachel had promised *her* mum that she'd come home for lunch and chill out for a bit (Mrs Riley was taking the proper meals and rest advice very seriously); TJ had promised *his* mum that he'd take Ellie to her extra tap-lesson with Mr Harper (cramming for the talent show final on Friday); and Megan had promised *her* mum that she and Naomi would always stick together (Naomi was currently in the neighbouring town of Westbay, while Megan was wandering aimlessly, yet again).

Now that the horror of shoe shopping was over and the twins were enjoying their afternoon nap – probably dreaming of bouncing tiny trainers off weary shop assistants' heads – I'd sneaked out to the peace of my den in the garden, where I was being driven *insane* by the locket's fastening mechanism.

I knew the sea salt had probably corroded it. (Could salt corrode gold? I should know, I guess, if I'd paid enough attention in chemistry.) But if only I could see what – if anything – was inside. Maybe that would help me know if this necklace really *did* belong to E for Elize. . .

"Don't just look at me – *help*!" I urged Peaches, sliding the locket under one of his fat paws, in the hope that with a quick flick of a claw, he'd snap the thing open and save me a barrel-load of frustration.

Peaches only frustrated me more, by contentedly tucking his paws underneath his furry belly, and gazing out through the small-paned window into our tangle of a garden. With the sun beaming in through the three tiny, uneven panes of glass, his green eyes took on an almost mosaic look – all speckles of olive and sunbeam yellow muddled together. It reminded me of something. . .

Leaving the locket on the desk for a sec, I got up and looked at the clutter of, well, *clutter* on the shelves of the den. Some of the mish-mash of stuff crammed on there were drawings and paintings and photos and candles and silly ornaments of mine from our old flat back in Kentish Town. And the rest of it was amazing trinkets I'd found in the den when me and Dad were first clearing it out. All of them belonged to Elize Grainger, who'd used this same small, brick building as her art studio, when she was a very old lady, a very long, long time ago.

But some of it was stuff I'd collected since I'd been here in Portbay; just your average beachcomber bits, like bright white shells and bluey black pebbles and . . . and a fragment of green and yellow tile that I'd found dusty and forgotten at the back of the fireplace in the ballroom of Joseph's House.

The rest of that tile, along with plenty of other matching tiles, was now in a big gallery room at the Portbay Museum, where lots of relics from the ballroom had been relocated and replicated, so that visitors got a sense of what such a grand 1800s room looked and felt like. In fact, the museum had rescued plenty of original features from Joseph's house, before time tick-tocked on and it headed towards oblivion at the hands of vandals and the demolition squad.

"Prrrrrp!" prrrrrped Peaches, turning his mosaic eyes towards me.

But maybe there were a few more pieces of Joseph's house and Elize's past that should be in the museum before it was too late, and maybe only *I* knew about them.

"OK, OK!" I said to Peaches, as his gaze filled me with guilt.

Taking the chunk of tile off the shelf, I walked over to the desk and began rummaging around for the photo I knew was in there somewhere. . .

"'Elize and Joseph, friends for eternity, 1841'. . ." the curator lady read, staring at the photo in her hand.

I'd taken that picture – of a hand-carved message in a window sill – a few weeks ago in Joseph's house, the first week I was here in Portbay, when

Frankie had come from London to visit. Me and Frankie had been so inspired by it that I'd carved, *Stella + Frankie, m8s 4eva, 2004* in the window sill of the den the next day.

"It's lovely! We'll certainly send someone to the old house to authenticate it, when we can spare them," the curator smiled encouragingly. "And of course this tile is just perfect; like a missing piece of the puzzle for our display!"

I felt kind of fuzzy inside when she said that, as if – nearly total strangers that we were – we had a friend in common (if you could call a house, and maybe two ghosts of people who once lived there, friends).

"The ballroom chandelier . . . it's still in one piece, kind of," I burbled, thinking of the missing chunks of crystal smashed by Sam's gang for "fun". "Couldn't the museum rescue it, before the demolition happens?"

"Of course, we'd love to. But it's a very large, very complicated, very expensive piece to move," the curator lady said sadly. "We just don't have the kind of funding to make that happen, I'm afraid."

I was so disappointed that a pain seemed to burn in my chest, but I was hardly surprised. The museum gift shop consisted of a bunch of postcards that were probably printed in the seventies, and a few tea towels painted with an artist's impression of the headland at Portbay, pre-caravan park. Together, I couldn't imagine them paying enough to cover the tea and coffee in the curators' staff room, never mind funding the delicate removal and repair of the grand chandelier.

"And as for the locket . . . well, I have to say that it *does* look as if it's quite old. But it could belong to any day-tripper with the initial E from the last hundred and fifty years! I really think your best bet might be to hand it in to the police. . ."

That wasn't the answer I'd been hoping for. I'd wanted her to say, "A-ha! Our historians here have this special antique locket-opening tool – let's see what's inside, and perhaps it'll be of phenomenal historical importance!"

Fat chance.

Disappointment must have been plastered all over my face, because the very nice, but not very enthusiastic curator lady suddenly came out with a suggestion.

"You enjoyed looking at the Grainger family portrait last time you were here, didn't you?" she said.

I had. Mainly 'cause I got to see Elize Grainger aged ten, with her best friend Joseph – the family's black servant boy – in the background.

"Well, I think you might like to see a painting we've just had donated from the estate of a local resident who died some time ago. . ."

I wasn't *completely* sure what "estate" meant (maybe just a posh way of saying "stuff"?), but I couldn't *wait* to see a new painting, if it had something to do with Elize Grainger. I had two images of her so far – the bright-eyed vision of her aged ten in the family portrait here, and an old photo from a newspaper in the 1930s, where the local press were celebrating her hundredth birthday, in her retirement cottage. That was very special to me, since it was taken in the garden of our house, with Elize posed by her easel, a watercolour of a fairy (the one I'd found during the den clear-out?) in front of her.

"Follow me, please. . ."

I followed, so excited that I knew if I spoke, my old stammer might come creeping in.

"Here we are!" the curator lady announced, as we walked into some strip-lit backroom that the public never got to glimpse. "Can you see the resemblance? We estimate from the shop-front style that it's from around 1850. Presumed local, but who knows where exactly."

I'd expected to see a version of Elize Grainger's pale, perfect, ivory-tinted face. Instead, the painting I was gaping at was of a young black man, maybe in his twenties, wearing a thick, cloth apron. Behind him was an old-style shop, with a blinkered horse shackled patiently to a cart in between them.

"We think it might be Joseph. Of course, no one knows what happened to Joseph, after Mr Grainger died and left him enough money to leave service and set up on his own."

I didn't know the term "leave service", but I got the gist. I already knew that Joseph had moved away from the house he'd served in from the tender age of ten (i.e. three years younger than *me*).

"As I say, the person who donated this painting died, which is very sad from the point of view that we've no one to ask about the history of it."

"Wow. . ." I murmured, feeling a sense of déjà vu ripple through my mind.

My grandad Eddie; that's who I was suddenly thinking of, or rather the one photo I had of him – aged nineteen and madly in love with my nana Jones. Joseph in his coarse work apron and

Grandad Eddie in his bomber jacket ... they didn't look alike, and they didn't dress alike, but they had plenty in common, these boys born a century apart. Both black, both originally from Barbados, both lost in the swirls of history, no one knowing where they ended up and what they ended up doing with their lives. . .

"Are you all right, dear?" asked the curator.

I wasn't totally all right. A huge weight of sadness was pressing on me, more uncomfortable than Peaches sleeping on my chest in the night.

"It's a bit dusty. I've got allergies," I said, making excuses for the wateriness that had crept into my eyes.

You know, plenty of people like mystery stories, but I wasn't sure if *I* liked them. The trouble with real life and mysteries is that sometimes in real life, you *never* find out the ending, and I was pretty sure I'd never find out the ending of Joseph's story, if the local townspeople hadn't already, *or* Grandad Eddie's, since neither Nana Jones nor my mum had managed to.

All of a sudden, I had the strongest urge to get out of the museum and into the fresh air. I wanted to see bouncy castles, Mr and Mrs Mystic Marzipan making balloon warthogs and wildebeest, rubbish human statues, and the sweet-toothed psycho seagull stalking unsuspecting holidaymakers for their candyfloss.

'Cause the best cure for sadness is definitely a dollop of silliness. . .

Chapter 8

The pink and green obstacle

Or maybe the best cure for sadness is toffee.

"Take another. Actually, take a handful and share them with your friends later."

For a second, my brain went *be-doinggg!* – how did Mrs Sticky Toffee know I was on my way to meet everyone? Then it dawned on me that I was being paranoid (as usual). Seeing my friends later – it was just a turn of phrase.

"Thangyooo," I mumbled, my back teeth glued together with gorgeous, buttery-sweet goo.

I'd just left the museum – the locket draped round my neck for safekeeping – and was heading towards the Galleria, where I'd arranged to meet Rachel etc. So much for looking for stuff to cheer me up on the way. Staring at the bouncy castle hadn't helped (the shrieks of all the little kids were too shrill); Mr and Mrs Mystic Marzipan – and their balloon animals – must have been on a long lunch-break; the rubbish human statue was standing surprisingly (and boringly) still; and the sky contained only a few standard, swooping, non-psycho seagulls.

So it was official: *nothing* had got me smiling, as I ambled along the prom, deep in thought and eyes fixed on the sea – till a pink and green obstacle blocked my way.

"Dear, dear. My little friend from London isn't looking too happy today!" she'd instantly chattered. "Here, have a toffee."

And now she was forcing more toffees on me, and I couldn't tell her about seeing Joseph's painting and how it had made me strangely sad, for the simple reason that my jaws were welded shut.

If Mrs S-T just gave me a second or two, then I could tell her all about it – and I really wanted to, seeing as she was the one who'd pointed me in the direction of the house and Sugar Bay in the first place.

"You and your friends should make the most of the Gala Week. *That'll* cheer you up. There're lots of lovely things going on," Mrs S-T chattered on. "There're so many performers and shows and exhibitions happening."

I wanted to say, "Yes, I know", but as it would just come out as "Eh-i-o", I decided to opt for a simple nod instead.

"They're holding super talent shows down here at the beach, you know."

"Yes, I do know, and my friend Rachel is entering it tomorrow," would have probably sounded something like *gargling*, so I just had to nod in reply again.

"I didn't see it yesterday, but apparently the most adorable little girl won."

Desperate to join in this one-sided conversation, I tried to chew like crazy, but it was like trying to run through thigh-high mud.

"So I popped down to watch today, and it was very entertaining, although I wasn't particularly enamoured by the winner. Some young girl only about your age, dear, in the most *awful* outfit," said Mrs S-T distractedly, as she stuffed the rustling bag of toffees back into her tiny handbag. "I didn't know you could get shorts that short. And where on earth do you buy bras with sequins on them. . .? Anyway, she was dancing in the most dreadful *wriggling* sort of way, as if she was desperate to go to the toilet! But there were plenty of people cheering – and wolf-whistling for her – so what does a silly old lady like *me* know!"

If I'd tried to answer at all just then, I might

have started choking and spluttering, and Death By Toffee would have been too silly a headline in the local paper.

Good grief – had Kayleigh entered *again*? Was that allowed?

"Must dash, dear," muttered Mrs S-T, as she snapped the clasp on her handbag shut and slid it on to her arm. "The Portbay Youth Orchestra are putting on a show at the garden centre, and bless them, you've got to cheer them on, even if they miss more notes than they hit!"

Oh, she was going – before I had a chance to ask what song Kayleigh had sung, and if most of the cheering and wolf-whistling had come from one particular bunch of loud and obnoxious teenagers.

"By the way, dear," added Mrs S-T, slowing her step just a little as she pootled off. "I think you'll find a gentle touch often works best!"

I rubbed the locket between my fingers as she waved and walked off, but really I felt like rubbing my head.

When you met Mrs S-T, there were two things she was guaranteed to leave you with for sure – a pocket full of toffee and a severe dose of confusion. . .

Chapter 9

Badgering and bouncing

Outside Rachel's mum's shop, I could see Bob frantically scratching at some irritating flea hip-hopping around in his fur.

Meanwhile, *inside* Rachel's mum's shop, TJ (freed from Ellie-watch for a brief time, since their mum was coaching his sister for her next talent show appearance) was shuffling around uncomfortably, pretending he was a) fascinated by the Fimo lobster letter-racks on sale, and b) deaf and couldn't hear the bickering going on.

"Stella, *please* help me to convince my beautiful daughter that she can't hide herself away, just because of this . . . this condition she's got!"

"Stella, *please* tell my mother to leave me alone!"

I'd been dying to meet up with the others at the Galleria and blab about what Mrs Sticky Toffee had told me about Kayleigh and the talent show, but I'd walked in on a full-scale difference of opinion. Mrs Riley was good-naturedly trying to badger Rachel into entering the Gala Princess competition on Friday, while Rachel was growling like a cornered badger.

"Um. . . I don't think Rachel wants to do it!" I said shyly, finding it difficult to argue with an adult, even a super-friendly one like Mrs Riley.

"But it's like letting this *thing* get the better of you!" Mrs Riley turned to say to Rachel. "I know we have to be careful, but you can't let something like this rule your life! You're a lovely young girl and should be out there having fun!"

"*Mum*. . ." sighed Rachel, rolling her eyes to the mobiles dangling from the ceiling, "you're only bothered because the Style Compony sponsors the float!"

The Style Compony? Portbay's one and only dyslexic hair salon, if their badly spelt sign was anything to go by? What did they have to do with this? Rachel spotted me looking confused, and seemed glad of a reason to turn away from her mum and explain things.

"Mum's best friend runs the Style Company. And every year, they sponsor the float that the Gala Princess rides on at the finale on Saturday."

"Darling, it's got nothing to do with Sandra

and the salon," her mum protested. "It's just that you've ridden on the float every year since you were a little girl, as one of the Princess's entourage. . . I just thought it could be *your* turn to take centre stage this time, Rachel, sweetheart!"

Mrs Riley was looking at her daughter imploringly, batting her eyelashes and sticking her bottom lip out. OK, so for the first time, I could *possibly* see why Rachel found it hard not to snap at her mum sometimes. Easygoing as Mrs Riley came across, she did seem to veer between being cheerfully bossy and annoyingly childish.

"Tough. I'm not entering the competition and I'm not sitting on that stupid float this year either!"

"Don't be silly, Rachel! It's practically a family tradition! You and Sandra's daughters *always* do it."

"Let one of *Sandra's* daughters enter the Gala Princess competition, then!"

"Darling, April and Ashleigh have already *been* the Gala Princess. And let's face it, Amber's not exactly going to win it, now is she?"

In a nano-second, I was running through my memory banks, finding no matches for "April" or "Ashleigh", but instantly linking the name "Amber" to the lanky, grumpy teenage waitress in the Shingles café. Then my brain struggled to match *her* to the glam little blonde-haired woman who ran the hair salon and regularly walked her matching shih-tzu dogs on the beach in high heels. (The woman, not the dogs.)

So much for piecing together more of the town's population. Now I suddenly clocked that TJ had glanced up from the ghastly, mutant mermaid teapot he was holding and glowered slightly at Mrs Riley when she mentioned Amber. I'd never managed to get Amber to mumble more than, "There you go", as she thumped a burger down in front of me, but I knew TJ quite liked her, and obviously resented Mrs Riley's casually thoughtless remark.

A-ha – had Rachel learned some of her bad habits from her mum, as well as Kayleigh and co? I was just mulling this over when Mrs Riley's attention was grabbed by something outside the window.

"Well, hello. . . Now *there's* a very pretty girl who I could see wearing the Princess's tiara on Saturday!" she commented, gazing across the road at a couple of girls arguing over by the blue railings on the prom. "Do you know who she is? The other one is your new friend from the town hall yesterday, isn't it?"

Megan: it was Megan, sitting on the prom railings talking (arguing?) with her sister.

Like TJ, I stayed schtum, leaving it to Rachel to explain who Naomi was. Would she blurt out that she happened to be fifteen, and secretly dating seventeen-year-old Si, and that Naomi's parents would go through the roof if they knew?

"That's Megan's sister. Her name is Naomi," Rachel said instead, plain and simple.

It seemed that – like Megan with Naomi – Rachel had some misplaced loyalty to her brother Simon.

"Actually, Megan'll be waiting for us," Rachel told her mum bluntly, before stomping over to the door and just expecting me and TJ to follow her out. Which we did, of course, glad to be away from any more potential bickering.

"God, she drives me *crazy*," growled Rachel, spotting a minuscule gap in the traffic and speeding across the road, while I hurried after her, and TJ took hold of Bob's collar and followed us both.

Naomi spotted us first. She was so thrilled (not) to see us that she immediately turned and headed away.

"Was it something we said?" I joked with Megan,

who was sitting on the prom railing agitatedly drumming her fingers on the sun-warmed metal.

"She's just in a huff with me," said Megan, frowning two blonde eyebrows together in a furrow. "I mean, I REALLY want to go to this show with you guys tonight, but on the other hand, I feel SICK about lying to my parents. *Again.*"

"Can't you just tell Naomi that you don't want to lie any more?" asked Rachel, sounding very much on Megan's side, I was glad to hear.

"I don't WANT to lie again . . . but I sort of kind of said *yes* about tonight. Just this one last time. . ."

As Megan shrugged apologetically, she held up her latest bribe – a twenty pound note.

"You should have told your sister to bog off," said TJ brutally.

"Yeah," smiled Megan, "but then I wouldn't be able to treat my mates to a turn on the bouncy castle AND a hot dog, would I. . .?"

It didn't feel right, the idea of Megan spoiling us with bribe money.

But then again, at the mention of hot dogs, my conscience-free stomach started rumbling. . .

"So you made us up, and now we exist! Cool!"

snorted TJ, laughing so much with his mouth full of hot dog that I worried he might dribble ketchup out of his nose.

But he was making some kind of sense. As we bumbled around the beach, noseying at the sand sculptures that had been done today (a not very fearsome shark won a first-place flag), and headed towards the bouncy castle in the car park, Megan had told us more about the cover stories she and Naomi had come up with for her parents this last week and a half. They'd invented a bunch of mates around Megan's age, that Megan and Naomi had "met" on their first day, and "hung out" with ever since.

OK, so at first, Mr and Mrs Samson hadn't been a hundred percent keen on the idea of their daughters disappearing off all day, every day. But then it dawned on them that the girls were perfectly safe together (ha!) with a group of thirteen-year-olds for company (ha! again), which left them to get on with their hobby of hiking, which turned out to be much more fun now they didn't have to drag two reluctant teenage daughters around with them.

They might have relaxed about Megan and Naomi disappearing during daylight hours, but they hadn't been too happy with the fact that their daughters were now staying out with Megan's "friends" sometimes in the evenings too. Naomi – as the oldest sister – had had to do a *lot* of reassuring to convince their folks they'd be fine (what a joke!).

Listening to all that, it made me mad for Megan. But she told her stories like it was all so funny that I ended up laughing as much as she and Rachel and TJ did. Especially when it came to the punchline: i.e., who knew her imaginary mates would turn out to be a) real and b) *us*?

"OK, bouncy castle time!" Megan announced suddenly, checking her change as we ambled over to the attractions.

"Nope – no dogs," said some cheerless attendant, as Bob raced towards the pay booth ahead of us.

"Well, *yeah*," TJ laughed, grabbing hold of Bob's collar. "Who ever heard of a bouncy castle for *dogs*?"

I loved the idea. A pet bouncy castle, where the Bobs and Peaches of this world could *boing* around – perhaps with mittens on to protect the rubber from punctures.

"Very funny," said the humourless, as well as cheerless, attendant. "Anyway, this is just for kids under ten, so the dog and you girls can't come in –"

He was gesturing at Bob, me, Megan and Rachel.

"– but *you* can, kid."

I could see the muscles clenching in TJ's (thirteen-but-small-for-it) jaw. *How* mortifying must that be. . .

"Forget it!" said Megan brightly, linking her arm into TJ's. "Let's all go get a Coke or something!"

Good for Megan.

Two minutes and four Cokes later, the heat of embarrassment was beginning to fade from TJ's cheeks.

"So . . . you're WELL up for the talent show tomorrow morning, eh, Rachel?" Megan said, slurping through her straw.

"I guess so," nodded Rachel, thoughtfully tucking a dark chunk of long, straight hair behind her ear. "I sang it OK at the café, so maybe it'll be all right. . . And if I don't feel like it, I can always back out."

"You can't back out!" blurted TJ. "It'll be fun!"

"Easy for *you* to say," snorted Rachel. "You haven't fallen flat on your face in front of a whole audience lately, have you?"

I suddenly felt for Rachel. . . It must be *terrifying* for her to imagine putting herself in everyone's line of focus again, so soon after her v. public seizures.

"Um . . . can't you do something too, just to keep Rachel company?" Megan suggested, staring hard at TJ.

"Well. . . I guess I *could* enter. I mean, I can *sort* of juggle – I've been getting lessons. . ." he said reluctantly.

Lessons from Mr and Mrs Mystic Marzipan, to be precise. I was smiling at the memory of how bad he was when I realized that Megan was staring at me too. . .

"Me?! I can't do anything!"

"You've got to be good at *something*, Stella. EVERYONE'S good at *something*," Megan grinned.

The only thing I knew I was good at was stammering when I was nervous. But before I could say that and get some sympathy, TJ had annoyingly butted right in.

"She can do cartoons – caricatures! She can do them really fast, can't you Stell?"

I hadn't drawn any caricatures since I was in

London – except for the one I'd done of Mrs Sticky Toffee. Since then I'd been getting into my ninja fairies – weird little hybrids of Japanese animation and old-fashioned Victorian painting like the kind Elize Grainger specialized in.

"Wow . . . you've GOT to do that!" said Megan, sounding well impressed.

"Yeah, go for it!" TJ nodded.

"Please, Stella – I won't feel so alone tomorrow," said Rachel, her pretty brown eyes all pathetic and begging, much like her mum's had been in the shop earlier.

However encouraging they were trying to be, there was only one answer I could give them.

"Er . . . yeah. Whatever."

Urgh.

How had *that* happened? One minute I was stroking the locket round my neck thinking "NO", and the next my mouth had turned traitor on me. . .

Chapter 10

Escape from the rainforest

What an action-packed day I'd had so far.

First, I got the chance to check out one of the Seaview Holiday Homes, then we were metal-detecting, followed by shoe-shopping hell with Mum and the twins, a disappointing *and* at the same time interesting visit to the museum, a brain-swirlingly confusing chat (plus sweets) with Mrs Sticky Toffee, witnessing Naomi in a full-on strop on the prom . . . and now I was hanging out in a rainforest. (Sort of. . .)

Actually, here are some facts about rainforests:

- *More than twenty percent of the world's oxygen is produced in the Amazon rainforest.*
- *Rainforests used to cover about a seventh of the world's surface, but they're being chopped down so fast that they could be wiped out in fewer than forty years.*

- *Experts reckon that the planet is losing thirty-five species of plant, animal and insect life per day, thanks to the rainforests disappearing.*

Now here are some facts about *The Roar of the Rainforest*, TJ's mum's play:

- *It was hard to tell it was set in a rainforest, as TJ's mum had gone for a modern look, with an empty stage and a black backdrop.*
- *It was hard to figure out if there was a plot, as all the characters just came on and did dramatic speeches or made animal noises.*
- *It was so bad it made your toes curl.*

"Hey, what's *he* supposed to be?" whispered Rachel, squinting at the man dressed all in black, creeping around the stage.

"Rotten?" suggested TJ, setting me and Megan and Rachel off on a bad case of the stifled giggles.

Actually, all the actors were dressed in black (to match the backdrop?), which made it hard to work out whether they were a sloth or a macaw or a ring-tailed lemur. In fact, we only knew that the actors were supposed to be stuff like sloths or macaws or ring-tailed lemurs because we'd looked at the list of characters in the programme before the lights went down.

"But what's he *really* meant to be?" I asked, once I trusted myself to speak without sniggering.

"He is. . ." muttered TJ, bending over in the dark and scouring the programme. "A lion. I guess he's the one who's going to roar, or that wouldn't be in the title."

"But do lions *live* in the Amazonian rainforest?" Megan murmured. "I thought they just hung out on the plains of Africa. . .?"

"Maybe *this* lion came on his holidays and liked it so much he stayed!" said TJ, grinning along the row of seats at us all.

"*Shhhhh!*" shushed someone from behind us, as me, Megan and Rachel struggled with the giggles again.

After a few moments of deep breathing and pressing nails into our palms, we got ourselves back together. I'd just managed to tune out of a particularly dull speech by the lion guy, and was thinking that I was *positive* that I'd watched a programme about how ring-tailed lemurs only live in Madagascar (i.e. *not* the Amazonian rainforest), when TJ's mum pounced on stage, teeth bared and hands held up like claws.

I knew from the programme that she was meant to be a panther, but she looked more like Gollum from *Lord of the Rings* about to hang his washing out.

"*Shush*!" shushed the person behind us again, as my sniggers spread down through the row, till all of us – *especially* TJ – were not-very-silently cracking up.

Here's another fact about *The Roar of the Rainforest*:

- *By the time the lights went down for the second half, there were four less people in the audience. . .*

"What are you going to say to your mum? Are you going to tell her we sneaked out at the interval?" I asked TJ, now that we'd escaped from the rainforest and could talk at a normal level.

"Are you kidding?" laughed TJ, pulling on his hooded top.

"But won't she expect you to know what happens at the end of the play?" asked Megan, as she jumped two steps down, one step back outside the town hall.

"She's got a copy of the script at home. I'll read

that before she gets back tonight. That's if Bob hasn't eaten it – he doesn't like being left on his own too much."

TJ had looked strange this evening – like he was missing an arm or something – without Bob *or* Ellie tagging along. Ellie was off for a sleepover at a friend's for the night, while Bob had had to stay home alone, since dogs aren't generally welcome at stage and theatre shows. (Bob would have probably liked the play more than us, though; he could have joined in with all the howling and roaring going on.)

"Hey, what time tonight are you supposed to be meeting Naomi again?" I asked Megan, watching from the pavement now as she finished off her two-hops-forward-and-one-back routine.

"Not for another half-hour yet. Wow, this square is so big and empty! It's PERFECT for. . ."

The word "cartwheeling" got lost in a mumble as Megan took herself off in a human spiral or six.

"Well, my dad isn't expecting to pick me up for ages," said Rachel, keeping a wary eye on Megan but resisting saying anything negative about her, "so why don't we go to the Shingle café and get a milkshake or something?"

"Yeah, why not," shrugged TJ, shoving his hands deep in his jeans pockets. "They're running karaoke nights all this week, remember, so it could be a laugh!"

At the mention of something to do with singing, I realized I'd forgotten to tell my friends about Kayleigh winning the talent show today.

"Guess what?"

I'd no sooner started up with my revelation when a loud "AAARGH!" interrupted me.

Ouch. Cartwheeling into that lamppost must've *really* hurt. . .

"THAT WAS FANTASTIC!" Pete, the owner of the Shingles café, boomed through the mike, as some holidaymaker took a bow to much applause. "SO WHO'S UP NEXT?"

"Are *you* up for it, Rach?" asked TJ, as the four of us crammed round the only free (two-person) table in the place. "It'd be like a warm-up for the talent show tomorrow!"

"Give us a second – we just got here!" laughed Rachel, wrestling a chair just far enough back to sit down on.

The Shingles café was only five minutes' walk from the town hall normally, but it had taken us a bit longer to get here tonight, 'cause of Megan's limp.

"Are you OK, Megan?" I checked with her. "Shall I get you a stool to put your leg up on?"

"No – I'll be *fine*! It's just a couple of bruises!" said Megan brightly, though I could see her wincing as she tried to manoeuvre her knees under the tiny table.

"Maybe you should get your mum to take a look at it when you get back to the carava— oh!"

Glancing up at the sound of Rachel's surprised "oh!", my gaze landed on a packed table at the back, where Kayleigh was rolling her eyes in a fake reluctant way as Brooke and Hazel clapped and whooped to encourage her to get up and take the mike. Then with a dramatic push of her chair, Kayleigh was on her feet, shooting a cocky, "I'm so popular" smug grin our way.

Rachel would've been devastated – if she'd noticed. But I'd got it wrong – her eyes *weren't* on Kayleigh and co at all. . . Instead, she was staring over at another packed table altogether. And her mouth was the same shape as the "oh!" she'd just squeaked out.

"It's Naomi!" said Megan, putting Rachel's surprise into words.

Naomi and *Si*, to be precise. . . They were at

two tables at the back of the café that had been rammed together, to make enough room for all Si's arty, rock crew, which included a straight-faced Tilda, the girl who always wore ballet tutus. The others in the crowd were much cheerier; in fact, they were cheering Naomi and Si as they both got – slightly unsteadily – to their feet.

And with a bit of a staggered, giggly run, the two of them were on the karaoke spot, clutching the mike between them.

"Check out Kayleigh!" sniggered TJ, pointing out Rachel's evil ex-friend, as she stopped dead, beaten to the mike and left standing stranded halfway between the karaoke "stage" and the table, looking like a complete dork.

Great!

I couldn't think of anyone I'd rather see humiliated like that. . .

Not that Kayleigh backtracking with a (pink) face like thunder had even registered with Rachel – she was too busy frowning at her brother and his giggling girlie.

"Si *never* comes here. What's he doing? He always says this place is way too naff, full of day-trippers and schoolkids!"

Well, if Rachel thought *that* was weird, it was

about to get a *whole* lot weirder. . .

"He's going to *sing*?!"

Oh, yes, Si – and Naomi – were most definitely going to sing. Either that, or they wanted an unusually close look at the microphone.

"*Si* doesn't sing!!"

Well, he did now. Him and Naomi were belting out a version of Coldplay's "Yellow", with about as much volume and lack of charm as fans at a football match.

"Since *when* did Si like Coldplay?!" Rachel asked no one in particular (not that anyone more than ten centimetres away would be able to hear her above the sound of the backing track and yelled lyrics).

I wasn't shocked like Rachel, but I *was* kind of intrigued to see such ultra-trendy, über-cool people as Si and Naomi happily make fools of themselves. The last time I'd seen someone staggering around and singing that rowdily was this old drunk guy that used to hang out at Kentish Town tube station, near where I used to live, with only his trusty can of lager for company.

Oops. . .

Had I just hit on something?

Were Si and Naomi *drunk*. . .?

Chapter 11

Frazzalated

I was feeling *so* sick.

Measles, chickenpox, migraine, gastric flu, gout, yellow fever, dengue fever, bubonic plague. . . I didn't know what some of those illnesses were, but I knew I'd rather have had all of them together than do what I was just about to do.

And that was to go on stage with my big notepad and draw – in front of the entire population of Portbay (it felt like), as well as a zillion holidaymakers. I was having trouble stopping myself wobbling into a full-on body tremble, so who knows *how* I was supposed to keep my hand steady enough to draw caricatures.

And worse still, the person I'd planned on drawing – since she was already a bit of a human cartoon – hadn't even turned up yet, and heat three of the talent show was just about to start. Even *worse* than that, the person I was planning to draw who hadn't turned up yet was the *very*

126

person who'd persuaded me and TJ to enter in the *first* place. . .

"Where *is* Megan?" I mumbled to TJ and Rachel, who were standing either side of me in the queue to go on stage.

"Maybe her leg got worse. Maybe it fell off," suggested TJ, as he practised his juggling, with fancy balls borrowed from Mr and Mrs Mystic Marzipan.

"She texted me last night, and she didn't mention anything about her leg being worse. . ." I muttered, too stressed to get TJ's jokey remark.

Mind you, Megan's leg falling off would have been the least of her troubles, by the sound of it. It had taken her for ever to beg Naomi to leave the café (and Si) and go back to the caravan before their parents wore out the battery on their mobiles calling them. (Naomi kept hers switched off, and poor Megan had to keep pacifying them and saying they were on their way, with her nose growing Pinocchio-style with every repeat of the lie.)

I was already in bed – trying to sleep but fretting about the talent show – when I'd heard Megan's text bleep through. At first, I'd thought it might be Frankie, 'cause she's the only one of my old buddies who might text so late.

Hi, it's Megan, I'd read on the illuminated display. *Got in BIG trouble with M+D.*

Cos u were so l8? Or cos of the state Naomi was in? I'd keyed back to her.

I'd waited a little while in the dark of my room, the only light coming from my phone, the moon and a pair of slowly blinking green eyes. And then her reply blinged back.

Tell 2morrow. Must go – N says sound of me texting is doing her head in.

Wow, Naomi must have been feeling really ill (with booze?) if a few soft bleeps hurt her head that much. Still, if she was a bit drunk, she couldn't have hidden that from her parents, could she. . .?

But back to today. As much as I was worried about Megan – and wondering why exactly her mobile was switched off this morning – I was worried right now about *me*, and the total fool I was about to make of myself.

Uh-oh . . . and I might also be worried about Rachel.

"Are you OK?" I asked her, noticing how pale and quiet she'd gone.

"I don't think I can do it, Stella!" she said faintly.

"Do you feel ill again?" I asked in a panic.

Beside me I heard the thump-thump-thump of three juggling balls being dropped, and TJ mumbling something about getting a chair.

"I feel fine – just now," said Rachel, with a nervy shrug. "I just worry about getting up there in front of so many people. It was OK in the café, but this is just a bit too big. . ."

I understood *exactly* how she felt. If *I* was feeling nervous and worried, then how bad must it be for Rachel?

No, this had been a rotten idea all round, and we just needed to get out of this stupid queue and. . .

"Welcome to the third and final heat of the talent show, ladies and gentlemen, boys and girls," Mr Harper the librarian's cheery voice boomed close by. "And as there're a lot of terrific acts to get through, I'd like to get the first to you straight away. A big hand please for – let's see who we've got – a little lady here with a big drawing pad!"

What?! There'd been a *ton* of people in the queue ahead of me. Where had they all gone? It seemed that in the couple of seconds I'd been seeing to Rachel, they'd all had a fit of nerves and shuffled to the back of the queue, leaving me in full view of Mr Harper. I glanced around for help from TJ, but he was still off trying to find some water, or a chair or whatever for Rachel.

"STELLA!" I heard a sudden shout close by. "Stella, I'm HERE!"

A pink-faced Megan was hurrying towards me, thrusting her way through the contestants. "God, that was *close*. You're getting called on stage, aren't you?"

Frazzled was too small a word. I was completely *frazzalated*. Mr Harper was still trying to wave me on, saying something about not being shy, and Megan's sudden appearance had completely thrown me.

"I'm not doing it!" I told her, knowing that I was probably completely wild-eyed. I didn't care that Mum and Dad and the twins would be out there, or Mrs Sticky Toffee, I bet. I had a lousy act that I'd be lousy at, and it just *wasn't* going to happen.

"Do it!" Megan insisted, grabbing my hand. "It's not like it's an exam – it's just for fun!"

That was easy for *her* to say, I thought, as I felt myself unwillingly being guided on to the stage.

Let's see how much fun it was going to be when Mr Harper asked my name and I stammered, "S-S-S-Stella S-S-S-Stansfield". . .

Rachel looked fine – I saw her sitting with Mum and Dad, Jake and Jamie, and Ellie and Bob. They'd all waved like mad (well, maybe not Bob) when I got off the stage and scoured the audience's faces for them.

TJ was fine too. After winning the heat with his very funny juggling act – where he'd kept stopping and making jokes instead of actually *juggling* – he'd ended up being swamped by a flock of girl fans, none of whom seemed to care that he wasn't the tallest thirteen-year-old in the world.

"Sorry, what was your name again?" the young woman reporter asked me, her pen poised over her notepad.

"Stella. Stella Stansfield," I told her, feeling my cheeks pink up a little with pride instead of panic.

The reporter was going along the line of all the contestants, taking our details after the group photo we'd just posed for on stage.

"I liked your act, Stella – it was fun." She smiled. "Really different from what everyone else was doing."

"I couldn't have done it without Megan!" I said, pointing to my friend, who took a jokey bow.

And I couldn't have. Megan had taken the heat off me while I drew her by breaking out of her pose and clowning around every time I glanced down at the white paper that my marker pen was flying over. She'd even got me laughing, as I tried to order her back to her place. The audience were cracking up at her antics. Mind you, I got a pretty big "Oooooh!" and applause when I finally turned my A3 pad around once my five minutes were up. But Megan got them all in hysterics again by walking off stage on her hands.

I still hadn't had a chance to find out what exactly had happened with Megan's parents last night, or why she was so late today, but I guessed that could wait. I was still buzzing from the sound of the applause and the fact that I'd almost, kind of *enjoyed* myself.

"No, your caricature was excellent," the reporter insisted. "And it was a nice touch, the way you wrote your name out on the pad when the host asked you to introduce yourself!"

A nice touch? I think it was pretty inspired. Hurrah for my normally lame brain coming up with that particular brainwave.

"Um, thanks," I said shyly, while running my

fingers around the locket I still had draped around my neck from yesterday. "I guess I just—"

Tink!

It was a sensation rather than a noise. The feeling of a tiny spring sproinging open.

"The locket!" I murmured, dipping my chin down and lifting it up to my eye level.

"You're kidding!" gasped Megan. "You got it *open*? That's ACE! What did you do?"

"I don't know!" I laughed, my fingers trembling so much that I could hardly unfold the two halves of the gold oval. "I've been trying everything to get it to open, but this time I hardly touched it!"

Hardly touched it. "A gentle touch often works. . ." that's what Mrs S-T had said yesterday, when I hadn't a clue what she was on about.

Had she meant the locket?

Could she have meant the locket?

But *how* could she have meant the locket?

Those thoughts whirled around my head and shot straight out again, as soon as I saw what lay inside. A tiny frame of glass, holding a snip of hair. Hair that was black, with a tight curl.

"It's got to be Elize's locket! 'Cause that has to be Joseph's hair!" I said, feeling almost breathless with excitement.

"What's this? What've you got there?" asked the girl reporter, getting close and interested.

And so I told her; babbled the whole story of the last few weeks. Of course – being local – she knew about Sugar Bay and Joseph's house, but she didn't know the connection I had with Elize Grainger, living in the same house as her, discovering all her trinkets, unearthing the friendship she had with her family's servant boy, piece by piece, clue by clue.

"Give me a minute," said the girl, once I'd finished.

"What was all that about?" asked TJ, finally breaking free of his fan club and coming over to join us.

"The reporter – Stella just told her the story about Joseph's house and us finding the locket and *everything*!" Megan filled him in.

"And look at it now!"

I held up the locket in my hand for him to see. Semi-open as it was, it looked like a gold butterfly resting in my palm.

"Hair?" TJ squinted into it at first, curious and curiously unimpressed. And then he got it. "D'you think it's a lock of *Joseph's* hair?"

I nodded, but there was no time for any more explanation – the reporter girl was back.

"Listen, I've had a chat with the photographer, and we'd love to do a story about this for the paper. How about after lunch today? Can you meet us over in Sugar Bay? I'd need one of you to bring a parent so that—"

The rest of the details blurred in my brain. Or maybe I was nodding so hard that the words were just crashing about inside my tiny, over-excited mind. . .

Chapter 12

Oh . . . did I forget to tell you my secret?

Thursday afternoon: the plan.

Megan had gone back to the caravan, TJ, Ellie and Bob had gone to their flat, and Rachel (after checking in with her mum) had come back to mine for lunch. We'd all arranged to be at Joseph's house just a little before 2 p.m., when the reporter and photographer from the local paper had said they'd meet us.

After a conversation with Mum and Dad this morning at the talent show, Dad had offered his services as the "accompanying parent" (he'd given up some quality DIYing time to do this).

It was all excellent and fabulous and exciting. Or as Megan would say, GREAT! and BRILLIANT! and ACE!

Um, except for just *one* little problem. . .

I hadn't *ever* told my parents that I'd been to Sugar Bay, never mind explored inside Joseph's house. They looked pretty surprised when I blurted out a bit about it, with the reporter girl by my side. And then over lunch, I didn't have much choice *but* to tell them more – after all, they'd be reading all about it in the paper on Saturday.

"Well, it sounds very interesting! I can't wait to see the place!" Dad had said, before throwing a look at Mum that seemed to say, "Why has our daughter been keeping secrets from us?"

Call me paranoid, but it felt to me like Dad was more on a mission to investigate, rather than keep us company.

Then when we stopped the car in the Seaview Holiday Park (the closest you can get to Sugar Bay in a car), he'd gazed down at the beach from the headland and mumbled about being surprised by how remote it was.

I didn't like the sound of that much for a start. There wasn't an awful lot to be said on the way down, since you needed to keep your wits about you on the steep, scree path. So me, Dad and Rachel just concentrated on staying upright, rather than chatting. I managed a couple of waves, though, to TJ, Ellie and Bob, who'd beaten us down there. And to Megan too, though she couldn't exactly wave back, as she was cartwheeling across the sands.

"Check it out!" said Megan, cartwheeling now across the vast expanse of (rotting) wooden floor in the ballroom of Joseph's house.

"So . . . what happened last night – with your parents and Naomi?" I asked, warily keeping an eye on what was going on outside the glass-free window.

It made me somehow uncomfortable, watching the way Dad was chatting with the reporter girl, but at the same time eyeing up the house like the disgruntled bloke from the council building department who'd been in our cottage yesterday. . .

Megan, meanwhile, cartwheeled to a standstill, and stood herself up, pushing the hair off her face.

We had time for this quick catch-up, thanks to the fact that the photographer had forgotten a particular lens and was trudging his way back up to his car, and the reporter girl – after jotting down the story of the locket from us – waited impatiently, passing the time chit-chatting to Dad.

That left me, Megan, Rachel, TJ and Ellie mooching about the ballroom, under the gaze and glare of the huge chandelier. (Bob was outside, dozing in the overgrown garden, under the gaze and glare of the sun.)

"Well, I force-fed mints to Naomi all the way back to the caravan, so she didn't smell of cider any more," said Megan.

"Cider?" I muttered, not exactly (or remotely) surprised that Megan's sister was drunk – it was just interesting to know what she'd been drunk *on*. I wondered how her and Si had got their hands on the stuff though, seeing as they were under age (*well* under age, in Naomi's case).

"Yeah, they didn't go to the cinema in Westbay *after* all; they just got a mate of Si's to buy them cider and drank it on the beach all afternoon!"

"So, did your mum and dad suss her out?" asked TJ.

"Nope. They thought she was just feeling ill with a tummy bug – that's what she told me to tell them before she collapsed in bed," said Megan, her voice less manic than usual. "They sent me to bed too, saying they'd talk to me in the morning, which I knew would be bad. That's why I nearly missed the talent show this morning – I was getting a lecture about staying out late with my friends, and how wonderful a sister Naomi was for staying and looking after me, even though she wasn't feeling well!"

"Did you say anything?" Rachel frowned. "Like how it was all your selfish sister and my selfish brother's fault, and not yours?"

"I *wanted* to," said Megan, rocking back and forth on the spot, as if she was considering a comforting cartwheel or two again. "But if I'd said *that*, then I'd have had to tell them about *other* stuff, and *other* lies, and it'd have ended up with me blabbing on about the *whole* thing."

A bit like with me and Mum and Dad and Joseph's house. . .

Y'know, I really, *really* didn't like the way Dad was eyeing up the house as if he was looking at a giant *bear* trap.

"I've got a bad feeling. . ." I murmured, right before THUNK!, the psycho seagull dropped on to the nearest empty window sill – startling us all – and setting up the most mournful, head-tilting "*CAWWWWW. . .!*"

Chapter 13

The big berk makeover

I was banned.

Banned from going back to Joseph's house.

To think, my parents had been all excited at the prospect of their daughter getting a write-up in the local paper – till Dad copped a look at the state of Joseph's house. . .

"Stella, I understand why you found the place absolutely fascinating," Dad had said gently to me on the drive home. "But it's a condemned building, and it's been condemned for a very good reason – it's not safe!"

I couldn't talk to him – I was just staring hard out of the car window, willing the crushing pain of disappointment to ease from my chest.

The thought of never wandering through those strange, empty, sad rooms, imagining them bright and decorated and bustling . . . it was too awful. It was like the hurt of moving from our old flat all over again, like leaving an old life behind. Only in

141

the case of the old house in Sugar Bay, it wasn't *my* life I was leaving behind, but Elize and Joseph's.

"I'm no expert builder, but anyone can see that the roof's in a bad state – and the timbers of the floorboards and stairs are just ready to collapse. And then there's all the broken glass. I mean, the way you lot pull yourselves in and out of the windows . . . you just need to put a hand on a shard that's left in the frame and you could hit a major artery. And can you imagine how long it would take to get an ambulance crew to you? Then, of course, there's the. . ."

I zoned out for a second. It didn't really matter how many reasons there were or how real they all were. The bottom line was, I wasn't allowed back to the house.

". . .I'm sure as an older brother, you understand how important it is to protect Ellie from dangerous situations, don't you, TJ?"

Dad had been looking in the mirror when he said that. In my misery, I'd almost forgotten that the back seat of our car was squashed full of TJ, Rachel, Ellie, Bob and two toddler car seats. (Megan had wandered back up to the caravan park, having arranged to meet us later.)

"Um, yeah," TJ had mumbled.

"And Stella," said Dad, his voice extra gentle and understanding (which made it somehow worse), "I think you've always known how unsafe the house was, or you wouldn't have kept it secret from your mum and me that you were going there."

He was right. But piling guilt on top of misery just made me feel a zillion times worse, no matter how gentle and understanding a voice he used. . .

Spotting my misery, Mum and Dad kept up the guilt-inducing niceness all day. In fact, they were over the top nice about me going around to TJ's to watch a DVD in the evening, and dropped me off with a bulging Sainsbury's bag of munchies. But emotionally, I still felt *trampled*, as if I'd been in a fight with a herd of buffaloes and lost. Badly.

"Here," said TJ, handing me something.

I hadn't even noticed that he'd left the room till he came back in again. But then, I'd watched about the whole of a movie just now and not really been aware of the actors, the plot, *or* the toffee popcorn I'd been shoving in my mouth. I'd *sort* of managed some conversation with Rachel and Megan – Megan was worried about where and what Naomi was up to tonight – but my mind kept drifting to Sugar Bay.

"TJ!" I heard Ellie giggle. "You look *very* stupid!"

"Good! I was trying to!"

I glanced round then and saw that TJ was holding out a bundle of spangly stuff to me. I also noticed that he was wearing a floppy purple hat with floppy pink flowers on it, some clip-on dangling earrings, a fleecy white jacket that looked like a giant pom-pom, his jeans tucked into pink cowboy boots and yellow rubber gloves.

"Er, *why*?" I asked, looking him up and down.

"Because we're all a bit bored and fed-up, so I think we should hold our own version of the Gala Princess competition tonight. . ." he grinned at me. "We'll call it . . . the Gala *Muppet*! Mum's got a great collection of nuts clothes. Here, you look through this lot, Stella, and I'll go get some more!"

"*I'll* help! *I'll* help!" shrieked Ellie, jumping to her feet. "Can I wear Mum's shoes with the cherries on them, and her posh nightie. . .?"

As Ellie followed a stomping TJ out of the living room, me, Rachel and Megan glanced at each other. Megan was beaming from ear to ear, which made sense, since anything silly was right up her street. Rachel, on the other hand, curled further into the corner of the sofa and looked worried. Having unexpected seizures was one thing, but I didn't think she'd ever voluntarily made a fool of herself in her *life*. Like her brother Si, in her own way, Rachel was *way* too cool.

"This is going to be ACE fun!!" laughed Megan, pulling her sweatshirt off in readiness for her muppet makeover.

"But what's his mum going to think?" I fretted, holding up a beaded, pink, chiffon something, and hoping Mrs O'Connell didn't get back till really late from her drama show – i.e. till TJ had the chance to tidy this lot away again.

"Um . . . y'know, I think I'll just *watch*," said Rachel.

"*WRONG!!*" TJ's voice called through from the hall.

It took a bit of persuasion, but finally Rachel gave in – probably because she knew she stood out like a sore thumb from the rest of us fancy dress muppets.

"I hate you all," she said, staring at her reflection in the mirror. But there was a smile twitching at her mouth. And how could she fail to smile, when she was dressed up in a polka-dot-patterned, 1950s ballgown (worn *over* her T-shirt and Ellesse tracksuit bottoms), rollerboots (TJ's mum had tried and failed to get a part in a musical that featured skaters), and Ellie's deelyboppers?

"I wouldn't try tap-dancing in *those*!" joked Megan, pointing to the rollerboots.

"And I wouldn't try cartwheeling in *that*!" Rachel joked back, nodding at the floor-length, skin-tight leopard-skin tube dress Megan had wriggled herself into. For a tomboy like Megan, the look was very glam, specially since she had on a pair of black high heels and a feather boa too. But just when it had all gone a bit *too* glam, Megan had accessorized her outfit with a red-checked tea cosy from the kitchen, worn at a jaunty angle on her head.

My outfit was pretty fantastic: hiking boots, matching stripy, knitted beanie hat and scarf – and a full-on belly dancer's outfit that Mrs O'Connell had bought cheap at a car boot sale in case it came in handy for one of her drama group plays. (According to TJ, it never had.) The belly-dancer get-up consisted of a swirly, beaded, pink chiffon skirt, and matching glitzy beaded bra. (*Very* nice over the top of my banana yellow Topshop T-shirt.)

"Hey, who's this?" I said, sticking my bottom out and howling the chorus of "Can't Get You Out of my Head".

TJ, Rachel and Megan burst out laughing at my Kayleigh impersonation, but Ellie – wearing a purple silk nightie and circles of lipstick as blusher – was too busy wrestling her fairy wings on to Bob to pay us freaky teenagers any attention.

"So what now?" asked Megan, once we'd stopped giggling.

"Catwalk!" TJ announced. "I'll get the music on!"

And so, one at a time, we moseyed and shimmied (and skated) across the living room carpet to a soundtrack of some terrible, screechy compilation called *Rock Divas Rock!* that belonged to Mrs O'Connell. (TJ's collection of indie and hip-hop CDs wasn't *nearly* silly enough for the Gala Muppet competition.)

"OK, so who's our winner?" asked TJ – who'd doubled as celebrity muppet photographer – once we'd all gone down the "catwalk" at least five times each, since it was so much fun. "Here . . . write it down on a bit of paper."

After a few catches and misses, we all found ourselves with a piece of Ellie's colouring-in paper and a wax crayon. It was a tough decision – we were all fantastic muppets, in our own way. But for me, it had to be either Rachel, who'd really gone for it and done an amazing, pouting, Kate-Moss-gone-insane model look, or Bob, simply because it wasn't very often you saw a long-haired Alsatian fairy.

"OK! Time's up! Turn your paper round!" ordered TJ.

Rachel (on TJ's colouring-in sheet)
RACHEL!! (on Megan's)
Megan (on Rachel's)
Rachel (on mine)
Me (on Ellie's)

"Right, so Rachel it is!" announced TJ. "Can you stand up, please, Rachel? And can we have the winner's tiara?"

Ellie hurriedly pulled a silver spangly tiara off her nearby panda and handed it to her big brother.

"Rachel Riley, I now pronounce you Gala Muppet!"

It was a bit of a stretch for TJ to reach up and fix the pure plastic tiara in place. Rachel was taller than him anyway, and with the rollerboots on there was an even *more* yawning gap. I thought it was pretty considerate of her to sink her knees down a little to make it easier for him.

"Why, thank you, thank you – *whoa!*" said Rachel, fooling around as she straightened up, and struggling to keep her balance. "I'd just like to thank my stylists, and Bob the dog for not farting tonight, and—"

Rachel's speech sounded like it was going to be splendidly silly, but the insistent ringtone from Megan's mobile cut it short.

"God, what time is it?" said Megan in a panic, wriggling the stretchy tube dress high enough up on her hips to dig her phone out of her jeans pocket.

"It's . . . just gone nine," TJ told her, glancing at the clock on the mantelpiece.

"Naomi was meant to ring me at 8 p.m., to arrange where we'd meet up!" mumbled Megan, her voice edgy with panic as she wrested the phone out and stared at the display. "Oh, God – it's my dad!"

TJ dived over, like a prize-winning defender, and flung the volume dial of the CD player down to nothing.

"Um, hi, Dad! No, we're fine. You couldn't get through to Naomi? Um . . . well, maybe her phone's out of credit or something. Oh, is it? Oh, I'm sorry, we just forgot the time! Yeah . . . yeah . . . she's fine. I'm really sorry. No, it's my fault. . . Like I say, we were just having fun and forgot the time!"

As Megan grovelled, she pulled face after tortured face.

"NO! No . . . you don't have to come and pick us up!" she suddenly blustered in a panic, flashing her eyes wide and desperate at us.

"Er . . . remember that my mum said she'll give you a lift, Megan!" TJ called out suddenly, loud enough for Megan's dad to catch.

As Megan relayed that into the phone, just in case her father *hadn't* caught it, Ellie looked up at TJ in complete confusion.

"But Mum isn't here!" she said, in her innocent voice. "And she doesn't have a car!"

"Shhhhh!" TJ shushed her. "It's called playing for time!"

As soon as he said that, I think me, TJ and Rachel had the exact same thought. If TJ's mum had a car, then Megan's parents could expect her and Naomi back at the caravan park in approximately five minutes. And that was *never* going to happen, seeing as there was no Mrs O'Connell, no car, and – most importantly – no Naomi. . .

"WAH-WAH-WAH, WAH-WAH-WAH!"

That was TJ, doing a very strange thing – putting his hand over his mouth and shouting muffled nonsense through it.

"Hey, Megan!" he shouted next. "Mum's just called through from . . . the, er, *kitchen* to say that she's got . . . er . . . something to do first, so it'll be another half-hour, if that's OK!"

Megan – her glam dress hoicked up around her hips and her shoulders sagging as if the weight of the feather boa was getting her down – looked bemused . . . and then suddenly got what TJ was trying to do and snapped into action, relaying the info to her grudgingly accepting dad.

"That was BRILLIANT, TJ!" said Megan, pressing the end-call button and instantly pressing the speed-dial number for Naomi. "*Noooo*. . . It's still just her MESSAGE service!! Oh my Go— Naomi! It's me! Where ARE you? We are in BIG trouble if you don't call me back RIGHT *NOW*!"

Y'know, it seemed a bit thoughtless of Rachel to suddenly get out her own mobile and start fiddling around with it, when Megan was in the middle of such a major crisis.

Except I realized it was the *opposite* of thoughtless, as soon as I heard what Rachel was saying.

"Si. . . Si. . . Can you hear me? What's that music? Where are you?"

Me, TJ and Megan . . . we must have looked like the *strangest* human statues as we stood frozen in our bizarre fancy dress, listening to one side of a conversation and trying to guess the other side.

"*What?!* Well, the reason I'm *hassling* you is that I know you're seeing someone, and I know her name is Naomi, and I know she's with you right now. And I *also* know that you'd better get her round to my friend TJ's flat in a taxi in about ten minutes, or her parents are going to go *ballistic*!"

Rachel sounded tough, stern, and not-to-be-messed-with. (Just as well her brother couldn't see what she was wearing, or he'd never have been able to take her seriously.)

"'Cause she's the sister of my friend Megan, *that's* why!"

Megan might have been mega-stressed, but I could see the pink flush of (pleasant) surprise in her cheeks when she heard Rachel say that last bit.

"No, I will *not* give it a rest, Si! I never butt into your life, and I never blab to Mum and Dad about anything I know you're up to. But if you don't get Naomi here now, I'm going to tell them that you were drinking cider last night. Yeah, I was there in the café – you just didn't see me 'cause you were too drunk! Just like you probably are tonight!"

After a quick pause – when sense must have been sinking into Si's brain – Rachel started reeling off TJ's address.

"Ten minutes, right? And tell the taxi driver to wait, 'cause he's got to pick up Megan and then take them both to Seaview Holiday Homes. Got it?"

"Are you OK?" I asked, noticing that Megan had flopped down dejectedly on the edge of the sofa arm.

"It's just been a bit of a weird day. . ." Megan murmured, her tea cosy hat slip-sliding sideways and nearly parting company with her head.

"Tell me about it," I said, nodding in agreement as I thought of Joseph's house, and patted the head of the long-haired Alsatian fairy who'd just ambled over and was leaning on my leg.

"Urgh . . . *BOB*!" grimaced Rachel, flicking her flip-top phone shut with one hand while fanning her face with the other.

"Sorry," said TJ, as the overpowering smell of fartiness filled the room. "It's toffee popcorn – has the same effect on him as cat food."

Bob looked up at me with his big brown eyes and panted happily, unaware of the general nerves, excitement, guilt, gloom and stress we'd all been through today.

I didn't know about the others, but suddenly I wished I was just a happily farting hairy fairy. Life would be *so* much less complicated. . .

Chapter 14

Getting the blame (gee, thanks!)

Today was many things.

Today was Friday.

Today was the final of the talent show.

Today was the competition for the Gala Princess.

Today was Megan's last day in Portbay.

Er. . .

Well, *there* was a fact I'd kind of overlooked, till Megan mentioned it on the phone just now. She'd called to arrange for us to meet up at the Sea Stage and cheer on Ellie and TJ at the talent show final.

"God, Mum and Dad were SO not happy," she'd moaned to start off with, telling me about the "welcome" she and Naomi had got last night. (The taxi with Naomi in it had arrived at TJ's in five minutes, so Rachel must have done a *great* job of emotionally blackmailing her brother.) "I think they'd have liked to ground us – well, me, anyway, seeing as they thought it was all my fault – but since today's our last day. . ."

And that's when I felt like I'd been punched in the chest with surprise, as I sat there at the computer, phone in hand, Peaches lying purring between me and the keyboard.

The thing was, I'd got pretty used to this loud, entertainingly daft, surprisingly kind, madly cartwheeling girl over the past few days – I wasn't ready for her to leave *quite* yet.

"What?" I squeaked, making Peaches jump.

"My last day . . . we go HOME tomorrow! We'll probably leave around 10 a.m. Hope that gives us enough time to get a copy of the local paper and see that piece about US and the locket. . ."

The locket. I had it wrapped up in tissue paper in my drawer in the den. Maybe once the people at the museum read the story in the newspaper they'd suddenly be *desperate* to see it.

"But if we miss getting the newspaper, would you post it to me, Stella?" asked Megan. "If I gave you my address, maybe?"

"If you want to stay friends, maybe?" I knew was what she was *really* saying.

At that moment, before I had a chance to say "Yes of course", Peaches rolled back on the

keyboard, typing: 'bnm,ryyyyyyy5rffffff456780
9987rt5534cdeew3r4TYUIIIIIIII with his furry
back, *right* across the e-mail I'd planned on writing
to Frankie, just before Megan rang.

"No problem – give me your address. And your
e-mail address too!" I suggested, at the same time
giving Peaches a scratch under his chin to say
thanks for the reminder of the wonders of e-mail.

"BRILLIANT!" Megan blurted back breathlessly.

Hmmm. Would she e-mail in capitals too, I
wondered. . .?

"BRILLIANT!" Megan shouted out right now, as we
sat on the sands, with Rachel and a snoozing Bob,
cheering as Ellie took her bow (and disappeared
from view, she was so little).

Her version of "Everybody Wants to be a Cat"
was a bit different this time around. For today's
final, she'd chosen a very special, *streamlined*
outfit of pink leotard, pink tights, black tap shoes,
plastic tiara ("That was *my* Gala Muppet tiara!"
Rachel had said, all jokily petulant, when she'd
spotted it). Oh, and – nice touch – a cuddly toy
black cat under her arm.

She should have asked me if Peaches would've
done it. He might've miaowed yes – after all, I

could see him now, lounging by the edge of the prom, staring down at the stage, eyes half-closed against the noon-day sun and tail gently flicking.

Actually, the outfit and stuffed cat were *all* that was different about Ellie's performance. She still gabbled and tap-danced her way at hyper-speed through the whole song, despite Mrs O'Connell standing at the side of the stage mouthing, *Slower! Slow down!!*

Unfortunately, Ellie was so absorbed in what she was doing that she didn't spot her mum. In the same way as if I'd stood in the wings during *The Roar of the Rainforest* and mouthed, *Stop looking like you're hanging out laundry and act more like a panther!* at Mrs O'Connell, probably.

Still, the crowd went mad, cheering and whooping and "awwwww!"ing.

Apart from the bunch of people nearby who were *booing*. . .

"What *is* their problem?" I gasped, turning around, and not being particularly surprised to see Kayleigh, Hazel and Brooke all giggling at Sam and his baying, booing mates like they were the biggest genius comedians on the planet.

"They are all total morons, *that's* their problem," Rachel hissed venomously, throwing a narrow-eyed glare of hatred their way.

But you know something? Even though my blood was boiling, and I knew Rachel's was too, hissing nasty things about Kayleigh and Sam and that lot was the most either of us could bring ourselves to do.

But not Megan. *Oh*, no.

While Rachel was still mumbling her "moron" remark, Megan jumped upright and charged across a bundle of crossed and stretched out legs on the beach to confront . . . well . . . the *morons*.

"How could you *boo* a little five-year-old girl?!" we heard her shout at them, her slim face red with rage and her fists white with clenching. "Why don't you pick on someone your *own* size?!"

With that she turned to go, hearing the expected sniggers and fnars erupt behind her. But ha! Those sniggers and fnars were drowned out in a flurry of "Yes!"s, "Exactly!"s and handclaps from the audience members who'd been close enough to hear Megan's telling-off.

Megan didn't look back to see Kayleigh and Sam and everyone's embarrassment and confusion. She was too busy stepping towards us with a wide-eyed "can't-believe-I-just-did-that!" look on her face.

"You were *brilliant*!" laughed Rachel, practically

giving Megan a hug as soon as she was close enough to our beach-bum level.

"I can't believe I just did that!" Megan beamed out loud, chuffed and shocked at herself. "I just got so MAD at them I couldn't hold it in!!"

"Maybe you should try being like that with your sister!" I suggested.

Megan's face clouded over a little.

"I'd be too scared Naomi would stop talking to me. . ." she mumbled.

"I wouldn't worry about it," Rachel said with a casual shrug. "Simon's not talking to me today 'cause of that call I made to him last night at the party. But he'll come round eventually. He always does. Same as *I* do when he's bugged *me* senseless."

But now wasn't the time to trade stories of huffy siblings, 'cause Ellie had left the stage, to be replaced by a sibling of her own. And wow – the crowd went just as mad for TJ's juggling (and jokes) act as they had for his kid sister.

Before long, they were all cheering and whooping and "awww!"ing again. Athough the "awww!"ing they were doing for TJ *wasn't* because they thought he was cute, as in Ellie-cute, but out of sympathy because he'd – oops! – gone and dropped all his juggling balls, *just* as his jokes'n'juggling act had been going down a storm.

"Y'know, I think he did that deliberately!" I whispered to Megan and Rachel, a sudden realization pinging into my head. "TJ messed up his act so that Ellie could win!"

And Ellie probably *could* win, based on her high-speed, but highly adorable performance just now.

Of course, there was still one act to go. . .

And then it dawned on me that there hadn't been any more booing during TJ's turn. Was that 'cause of Megan's telling-off? Or because everyone seated around Sam etc. had shown how much they disapproved of their moron noises? Or was it just 'cause Kayleigh had had to leave her "best" (i.e. "worst") mates and scoot up to the stage, ready for *her* turn to perform?

"Please welcome back on stage. . ." Mr Harper boomed through the giant speakers on either side of the Sea Stage, ". . .Kayleigh, and her great rendition of Bay . . . Bayon . . . *Beeyonk*'s hit 'Crazy in Love'!"

OK, so Mr Harper hardly had his finger on the pulse of current(ish) pop music, but I didn't waste much time thinking about the mistake he'd just made, since practically the whole audience – perhaps with the exception of Mrs S-T over there by the ice-cream seller – knew that the singer was actually known to everyone in the western hemisphere and *well* beyond as Beyoncé.

And let's face it; whether Mr Harper called the singer Beyoncé, Beeyonk or Bouncy, my attention – along with everyone else's – was drawn to the girl strutting her way on to the stage just now.

"Can't she wear *anything* but those shorts and that Union Jack bra?" I wondered aloud, as Kayleigh (who'd obviously done a quick costume change backstage) bent over and pressed a button on her boom box.

Me, Megan and Rachel were transfixed with horror as Kayleigh confidently began an out-of-time, horribly jiggly dance routine to the opening bars.

"Oops, my phone," Megan suddenly muttered, reaching into her drawstring bag.

OK, so now it was hard to figure out who to concentrate on: Kayleigh looking like a complete pillock (in a spangly bra) on the stage, or Megan, turning a shocked ashen white as she listened to whoever was saying whatever on the phone to her.

I quickly nudged a stage-staring Rachel to take a look at what *I* was looking at.

"What do you MEAN, we're in so much trouble?!" Megan burbled, one finger now rammed in her ear to drown Kayleigh's warblings out and hear her own conversation all the better.

Rachel frowned prettily at me, and I shrugged back, completely in the dark as far as guessing what was going on.

"They found a half-empty bottle of *what* in our beach bag?!" Megan asked frantically. "Huh? But. . . But Naomi, how could you forget it was *there*? You KNOW Mum would have got the sandy towels out to wash them! *Huh?* You WHAT?! Naomi! PLEASE tell me you didn't say that! 'Cause if you said that. . . Naomi! What? No! *Don't* hang up on me! I need to know. . . Oh."

"WHAT!" me and Rachel blurted out in unison, probably sounding as loud and capitalized as Megan ever did.

"My mum found a cider bottle in the bag that me and Naomi keep our beach towels in. . ." Megan murmured in a numb-sounding voice.

"Uh-huh!" Rachel urged her on, since we'd

already sussed that bit.

"But when our parents hassled Naomi about it, she said it was MINE! That me and my *friends* had been the ones drinking cider yesterday!"

When Megan had confronted Sam and everyone, it seemed like all the blood in her body had rushed to her face. *Now* it seemed like every last drop had drained from her body, leaving her ghostly pale.

"Uh . . . you mean *us*? I mean, your parents think *we've* been getting you drunk or something?" I gasped, feeling the weight of unfairness wallop on to my shoulders and press me down.

"Yep," Megan answered gloomily. "And then Naomi told me that Mum and Dad are COMPLETELY flipping out and want us both back *straightaway* . . . except she had . . . some kind of *stuff* to do first, and that she'd managed to put them off, and that I should wait for a text from her telling me where to meet up with her!"

I felt a flurry of alarm. Rachel's almond eyes widened in alarm. Bob's ears flattened in alarm (or maybe that was just the top note Kayleigh had failed dramatically to hit).

"Omigod," whispered Megan to herself, "my mum is *so* going to kill me!"

"But won't she kill Naomi too?" I asked, frowning hard. As the eldest of the two, why wouldn't their mum come down hardest on Naomi for not setting Megan on the straight and narrow? (Even though being on the straight and narrow was *exactly* what poor Megan was doing the whole, boring, cover-up time.)

"No, 'cause Naomi's my stepsister, and Mum doesn't feel comfortable telling her off, since she thinks that's my dad's – I mean, my stepdad's – job. Since Naomi is *his* daughter."

Wow ... the fact that Megan might have wanted to be mates with her cooler, older stepsister suddenly made a whole lot of sense. Obviously that's why she was willing to land herself – and us – up to our necks. But Megan needed to realize that Naomi was pushing the sisterly (stepsisterly?) favours way, way, *way* too far. Like to the other-side-of-the-*cosmos* too far.

"Yeah, but –" Megan started to say, fumbling about madly for an excuse for Naomi's awful behaviour.

I didn't suppose Megan's lame excuses for Naomi were going to convince either me or Rachel, but then we all got distracted by a pretty unexpected sound.

"PPPPPHHHHHHHHHTTTTTTTT!"

That was one *very* loud farting noise, and it had nothing to do with Bob, for once.

Well, it wasn't technically a fart – it was more a bunch of raspberries, blown from a bunch of lads in the not-very-distant crowd just as Kayleigh was in the middle of one of her trademark bottom wiggles.

It was perfectly and noisily timed, so Kayleigh looked like she'd just done a woofer.

And before she could even clock who the culprits were, there came a shout of, "POOOO-EYY! WHO DID THAT? *GERROFFF!!*"

And then Sam and his mates (oh, yes it was them) cracked up in cackles of laughter that were so loud that everyone in the audience who hadn't already turned round to gawp at them did exactly that.

At which point, Kayleigh burst into tears and ran off stage.

"Wow. . . What an exit," said Megan, open-mouthed.

"That wasn't very nice," Rachel muttered, sounding almost sympathetic. "Still, I can't think of anyone who deserved it more!"

"Kayleigh didn't get it, did she?" I said, to Rachel in particular, thinking of her (recent) history with

Kayleigh and Sam and co.

"What?"

"She didn't figure out that boys like Sam are horrible all the time, and no one's safe, even their so-called best mates!"

As I said that, the irony hit me: that girls like Naomi were horrible *all* the time, and no one was safe, even their so-called best stepsisters.

"How*whooooo*?" whined Bob, all of a sudden waking from his snooze like someone had barged into his dreams and shaken him.

His hairy head swivelled round for a second, then his dopey brown gaze fell on something up on the prom. It was Peaches, arching his back into a stretch and strolling idly away.

"What? What's wrong?" asked Rachel, spotting me staring, but not what I was staring at – Peaches had just disappeared into the holidaying throngs.

Where was my fat, freaky cat off to? And why had Bob suddenly acted like he was tuned into Peaches' weirdo wavelength?

"And so the winner is . . . Electra O'Connell! Well done, Electra!" Mr Harper's voiced boomed into my thoughts.

Ellie! Ellie and her hyper-speed song had won!

"And don't forget, ladies and gentlemen, boys

and girls," Mr Harper shouted above the wild applause, "after a short break, the search for a Gala Princess will take place right here on this stage, so stick around!"

Who cared about the Gala Princess? Nothing could top the Gala Muppet competition last night anyway.

And right now, we had a small, tap-dancing winner to celebrate with. . .

Chapter 15

Bounce! Bounce! Hisssssss. . .

In Japan, they have a sport called sumo wrestling. It's where two really ginormous fat blokes go crashing into each other, and whoever falls over first, loses.

Oh, and they're in the nude. Practically. (Well, a weeny loincloth hardly counts, does it?)

Now a little piece of Japan had come to Portbay, just next to the bouncy castle. It was a sumo-wrestling ring, and for a small amount of money, anyone could put on a costume, become a sumo champion and bash bellies with other people in costume until they fell over.

"C'mon!" said one of the huge sumo wrestlers currently in the ring. "Have a go at me!"

"I can't. . ." mumbled the other sumo wrestler, looking totally forlorn.

"Go on! Charge into me! It'll make you feel better!"

Sumo wrestler number one (in the blue

loincloth) wasn't very tall, but he was very, very wide and round. He was standing in the middle of a plastic sheet, with a white circle painted on it to represent a ring, a grin on his face and his arms outstretched.

Sumo wrestler number two (in the red loincloth) was taller, but just as wide and round. She had her arms languishing limply by her sides, only they kind of stuck out at right angles, due to the general roundness going on.

"Don't want to. Don't want to hurt you," Sumo wrestler number two mumbled some more.

"You can't *hurt* me! That's what these suits are for!" shouted TJ (i.e. sumo wrestler number one), as he pointed to the inflatable, nearly nudey, fat-bloke suit he had on. "There's *way* too much padding for anyone to get hurt!"

Megan had been moping badly since the phone call from Naomi. Normally, she was like one of those happy-looking toy dogs you wind up that does back-flips every two steps. Now – as she waited and wilted for Naomi to call back – she was more like someone's lost teddy in the rain, all soggy and left stranded on a garden wall.

She had managed a wobbly-smiled "Well done!" at Ellie when we went up to hug her after the talent show, but perhaps it was just as well that Mrs O'Connell and Mr Harper had decided to whisk Ellie away for a mega ice-cream fest at the café to celebrate. If *we'd* gone with her, Megan's air of gloom and doom would've probably made Ellie cry into her sundae or something. After that, me, Rachel and TJ were all visibly struggling to think of a way to fill the time till Naomi deigned to get in touch and put Megan out of her misery. Then – *blam!* – TJ had come up with the sumo-wrestling idea. But so far, sumo wrestler number two seemed to be finding the game about as much fun as getting a filling at the dentist. . .

"I really don't think I can do this, TJ!" Megan whimpered forlornly, her troubled face peeking out above the blown-up blobbiness.

"Come on – just charge into me!" TJ roared, not giving up. "Pretend I'm Naomi!"

A-ha. A glint of something that *might* have been anger suddenly twinkled in Megan's eyes, I noticed, from the safety of the guardrail surrounding the sumo ring.

"Uh-oh," muttered Rachel. "Her nostrils are flaring!"

I guessed Megan was one of those people who

didn't get angry too often. I remember Frankie's mum (Aunt Esme) once saying that people who don't get angry too often tended to skip through life till it all got too much and then they'd explode. ("Like a bunny with a hand grenade," Aunt Esme had told me, nodding wisely.)

Well, Megan didn't so much skip as cartwheel, and that sumo suit didn't make her look much like a bunny. But I'd never seen her flare her nostrils like that, which was *kind* of worrying. . .

"*AAAAAAAAAARGH!*"

For a second, TJ looked terrified, and then I couldn't see his face any more because Megan had bumped big, fat, inflatable plastic tummies with him so hard that he went flying.

"Is he all right?" I worried, watching TJ's arms and legs flail around.

I was having to grip on tightly to Bob's collar as he started whining and fretting for his potentially battered and bruised master.

"He just needs help getting up. Look, Megan's there and – *oops*!"

Quick as a flash and with a grin a mile wide, TJ had grabbed Megan's offered hand and pulled her right down beside him, so they were both rolling about like turtles stranded on their backs. Even if the costumes hadn't stopped them getting up, their helpless laughter probably would've stopped them anyway.

"You and me next?" I smiled at Rachel. "I could pretend to be Kayleigh, if you like!"

"Absolutely not!" Rachel smiled back at me. "Anyway, I don't need to get any revenge on Kayleigh. It was enough just to see her face when her 'mate' Sam and the others made a fool of her. Maybe now it'll dawn on her how it felt for *me* – being dumped on by your friends, I mean!"

Y'know, I suddenly wondered if Peaches had pointed me in the direction of Megan for two reasons: 1) 'cause we'd become pretty good mates, and 2) to help rub those bad attitudey edges off of Rachel. Rach had been brilliant (BRILLIANT!) for the last few days, minus those flashes of snobbiness and big-headedness and sarkiness I didn't much like.

It was just a pity our friendship with Megan was going to end in such a weird way. It wasn't as if we were exactly likely to see her or her parents (or her awful sister) again after tomorrow, but I think we all felt a bit hurt that someone's mum and dad would go away with such a horrible opinion of us, as a bunch of under-age boozy kids leading their daughter astray. And much as we felt sorry for Megan being emotionally bullied into the lie, we didn't see why – scary as it would have been – Megan couldn't land her sister in it instead of us.

But then I guess it wasn't any of *us* who had to live with Naomi every day – maybe this was just the easiest way out. . .

"By the way, why's it so quiet round here, d'you think?" asked Rachel, gazing around at the distinct lack of queues at the sumo-wrestling ring, and the bouncy castle just beside it.

"Everybody's down at the beach, watching that whatchamacallit Princess competition!" the big, bulky sumo attendant guy called over to us, as he easily lifted TJ and Megan up by an arm each. "Hardly worth the bother staying open just now. My mate on the bouncy castle's closed up for an hour and gone to the pub till it gets busier again later!"

Hmm. A boozy guy watching heaps of kids bouncing up and down. If that didn't make his head swirl I didn't know what would. . .

"Shall we go along and check it out after this?" suggested Rachel, chucking her head back in the direction of the Sea Stage, where we could hear muffled intros from the host, plenty of music, and cheers from the crowd.

"Yeah, I guess. Anything to keep Megan busy," I mumbled, quickly checking the phone I was holding for her and seeing no missed messages or calls from the elusive Naomi. . .

A quick change out of sweaty sumo suits and the four (and a furry one) of us ambled back down towards the Sea Stage, where the Gala Princess competition must've been just about to wrap up.

"Let's sit *there* and watch," said TJ, pointing to the tall, semi-worn wooden beach breakers.

Other people had had the same idea. The breakers had tons of people perching on them, since the sands in front of the stage were so crowded. But there was a space there for us, with a not-too-lousy side view of what was going on.

"Here comes our last contestant of the day. Isn't she lovely?" said a smarmy bald man – the host, presumably – with his back to us and sort of blocking the view of whoever was looking "lovely" on stage. "What's your name, my love, and where do you come from?"

"My name is Svetlana, and I am from the Ukraine," said a girl with an accent who we still couldn't quite see.

For some reason, what Svetlana had just said

caused a whole blast of laughter from some people further up the breakers. Megan seemed oblivious – she was just staring at her mobile, willing Naomi to ring.

"How fascinating! And what are you doing here in Portbay, Svetlana?"

"I come to Portbay to open piercing salon!"

I hadn't been to any of these Gala Princess things before, but that didn't sound like the response of the average contestant.

Megan must have tuned into that last weird comment too, since she flipped her gaze up suddenly and frowned hard in the direction of the stage.

Rachel, meanwhile, had bent over and was glowering down the breakers, trying to suss out who was laughing – again.

"Um . . . a piercing salon. How, er, unusual!" the host guy bumbled. "Well, that's fantastic. Now would you mind doing us a turn up and down the stage, please, Svetlana, just to let the audience see how lovely you Russian girls are?"

"Sure. . ." Svetlana growled seductively into the microphone.

From further up the breakers came whoops and more laughter and wolf whistles.

"Hey. . .!" I heard Rachel mutter, her head still turned towards the breaker-perchers further down from us. "That's my brother and his mates!"

"And that's . . . that's *Naomi!*" gasped Megan, as "Svetlana" swayed and sashayed her way to the front of the stage, in the sort of exaggerated model style that we'd done last night for our own personal Gala Muppet competition.

"*Go*, Naomi! *Go*, Naomi! *Go*, Naomi!" barked the breaker crew down from us, confusing everyone in the audience who thought they were supposed to be supporting "Svetlana". I bent forward and – sure enough – saw Si balancing on the breaker whooping, while his mates cheered Naomi on. With the exception of that weird girl Tilda, who was staring at the low-flying seagull whirling above the crowds.

"She's taking the £%&*!"

Taking the mick – that's what TJ meant as he watched Naomi's cartoon swagger. But his version was a bit ruder. . .

"Thank you, Svetlana!" boomed the host, as the music was unsubtly faded out (i.e. turned down). "Can you please take your place backstage with the other contestants while the judges make their decision?"

The host did some burbling about how it would take five minutes for the decision and how we'd have some relaxing music while we waited. But while some awful female ballad crackled loudly over the sound system, all I could concentrate on was Rachel storming off to confront her brother.

"*This* is what Naomi 'had' to do?" said Megan, sounding stunned. "So she just wanted to lark about with her boyfriend and her mates, having a laugh, while I'm getting an ulcer *worrying* about what our parents are going to say to us?!"

"You've *got* to tell your mum and dad," said TJ, as he struggled to hold on to a suddenly restless Bob's collar. "Your sister's not just having a laugh with Si and that lot – she's having a laugh at *you*, the way she's acting!"

As TJ ranted, I could see Rachel arguing with her brother. Si looked a whole lot less than pleased to have his kid sister dissing him in front of his cool mates. And so he stomped off, tramping round the edge of the crowd and over to the far side of the stage, leaving Rachel staring after him, in the company of his stunned-into-silence mates.

"I can't help it. . . I just want to be friends with her!" I heard Megan try to explain.

"Yeah, sure," I said with a shrug. "But you're

only a friend if you're on the same side, and I think Naomi's on a side all by herself!"

It was the nicest way I could think of to say, "Naomi's a selfish moo." Megan got that all right; in fact, she looked like she might cry. She seemed a million miles away from that happy-go-lucky, cartwheeling nutter who'd crashed into me on Monday. Suddenly, Megan's relationship with her (step)sister had crashed completely and she looked kind of *crushed*.

"Look, Megan," shrugged TJ, as Rachel stomped up the sands to rejoin us. "You've *got* to tell your mum and – BOB! BOB! Come back, Bob!!"

But Bob was off. A blur of hairy dog-ness bounding across the sands and up the steps that led on to the prom. Before any of us had time to gasp, he'd disappeared from view behind the towering all-weather awning spanning the Sea Stage.

"We've got to get him!" TJ called out to me, Megan and Rachel, though we were already hurrying as fast as the slipping dry sand would let us.

Several slow, running steps later, we were all thundering up the stone steps on to the prom, gazing in the direction Bob had gone – and seeing nothing.

TJ, Megan and Rachel carried on running towards the beach car park and the bouncy castle, since that was the most likely route Bob had taken.

But I wasn't so sure. Maybe he'd crossed the road – the traffic was quiet-ish – and headed into town, or *home*, for that matter. Though why he'd want to do that when he was devoted to TJ I couldn't figure—

"Think it was a cat."

"Excuse me?" I asked, flipping my head around to see the old lady sitting on a bench, sharing pink candyfloss with a giant seagull.

"That daft big dog of your friend's – he was chasing a cat, I'm pretty sure of it," Mrs Sticky Toffee smiled at me, wafting her candyfloss in the direction of the others. "Better hurry and catch them up!"

I stood human statue-still for a second, wondering a) if I was going slightly crazy, and that was *bad*, or b) if Mrs S-T was slightly crazy and that was OK, or c) if Bob had gone completely crazy and started chasing imaginary cats along the beach. After all, outside of Greece, when did you ever hear of cats sunning themselves on the sands? Well, except of course for Peaches.

Peaches. . .

As this possibility started sinking into my muddled head, my legs made up their own mind and started running to catch up with TJ, Megan and Rachel. In the background, while my footsteps and heartbeat pounded, I could *just* make out the host on stage announce something.

". . .blah blah-de-blah . . . winner is . . . Svetlana!"

Svetlana/Naomi was obviously a popular choice as the Gala Princess, judging by the roars of approval.

"Uh, could Svetlana make her way to the stage, please?" I heard more clearly, after a few seconds.

"Has anybody seen Svetlana?" I heard the host suddenly ask almost mournfully, as I thundered along the pavement, with Rachel, Megan and TJ now in my sights.

Maybe they'd already seen Bob disappearing amongst the inflatables at the beach car park, but that's certainly where the three of them stopped up ahead of me, glancing all around, when an ancient silver (and rust-edged) estate car squealed to a halt right beside them.

In a twinkling of an eye, a man with silver-flecked dark hair and a woman with grey-blonde hair – who looked an awful lot like Megan – were standing in front of her, demanding to know what she was playing at.

"*Nothing!*" I heard Megan say, as my feet pounded on the pavement towards them. "I haven't done *anything*!"

The bouncy castle might have been closed, as was the sumo ring now, but loud chart music was still pumping through speakers tied to the surrounding lampposts. Up above the bouncy castle turrets, circling lazily low almost in time to the music, was a familiar-looking seagull.

"Oh, yes? Then what's this, then?" said Megan's mum, pulling a cider bottle out of her bag. "Don't try and pretend, Megan! Naomi's told us what's been going on, and what you and your friends have been getting up to. Well, I think your dad and me will have to have a word with their parents and let them know what—"

"There!" I said to TJ, Rachel and Megan, breathlessly pointing to the unattended bouncy castle up ahead.

Sure enough, Bob came scurrying from round the back, circling the inflatable castle like it was a giant sheep.

"Megan! *Megan!!*" her stepdad hissed angrily, oblivious to why we were all looking elsewhere. "We're *talking* to you, young lady! Listen to your mother when she's. . . Oh."

Oh, yes, "oh".

Oh – because the bouncy castle was not-so-slowly deflating in front of our very eyes.

Oh – because as the towers and walls deflated, the couple snogging inside – "Svetlana" and Si – came into full view.

Oh – because a plastic bottle of cider had rolled away from the heavily snogging couple.

"Oh. . ." mumbled Mrs Samson, staring and stunned into near-silence by what she was looking at.

What a lot of "oh"s.

But as the truth landed with a *splat* in front of Megan's mum and stepdad, "oh" seemed to quietly – and perfectly – sum up the situation.

"Er. . . I think we should all go back to the caravan and get this sorted once and for all," said Megan's mum, her gaze still locked on the obliviously snogging couple.

"Absolutely," muttered Mr Samson, about to stride forward and call to his elder daughter.

But Bob had beaten him to it and padded on to

the bouncy castle, stepping all over the smooching couple, making them bound apart in shock – just in time to spot their unexpected audience. . .

Only a few seconds later, it seemed, a pained-looking Megan was waving bye to us from the back of a hastily driven estate car.

"She *will* be able to say bye to us properly, won't she?" asked TJ, as we kept a discreet distance from the now-flattened bouncy castle, where Si was sitting with his head on his knees while Rachel knelt down and tried to talk to him. (From the way Si kept shrugging Rachel's comforting arm away, I guess he maybe blamed her somehow for Naomi being dragged away. Not fair of him, but not surprising, I guess. I hoped him and Rachel could make up again soon and have a laugh about the mountain of sweaty old socks huddled under his bed.)

"I *hope* so," I replied, not sure if that was going to be possible, in the circumstances.

"Hey, Stella, how d'you think a thing that size could've deflated?"

"No idea," I murmured, my gaze moving from the car speeding off towards the headland to the figure of a girl – in a tutu and black leather jacket –

stomping along the beach. Above her, a seagull swirled in low, elegant figures of eight.

Did I maybe smell the faint hint of jealousy and revenge in the air, care of that girl Tilda?

Nah . . . she was too far off.

Wasn't she?

"Hey, are you wearing that funny scent again?" TJ suddenly frowned at me.

"What scent?" I frowned back at him.

"It's like peaches and cream or something. Your whole house smells of it."

A-ha, so Peaches was still around here somewhere, probably lazily licking his fur and taking it easy after leading Bob (and us) here. 'Cause that's what he'd done, I was 99.9% sure.

For a millisecond – just a millisecond – I found myself *nearly* tempted to tell TJ just how freaky I thought my cat and several other beings in this town were (Tilda included), when a text message bleeped on my phone.

2moz – 10am, parade. C U outside town hall? Megan x

Well, it looked like Megan was determined to say bye to us properly, whatever complicated family mess was going on. . .

Chapter 16

Parading, pogo-ing and parping

Wow...

If someone told me that the entire population of North London had turned up on the streets of Portbay this morning, I might have believed them.

I'd never *dreamt* that I'd see the streets and pavements of this little town so packed. Gawping at the general crush here by the town hall, I was glad Mum and Dad had decided to wait with the boys down by the beach to see the end of the parade. At least down there it wouldn't be so manically crowded.

"It's like this every year!" said Rachel, being buffeted behind as people squashed forward for a better look at all the ornately decorated lorries and trailers rumbling by.

"That's why I left Bob at home," said TJ, struggling to see as enthusiastic big bloke dads barged by with little kids on their shoulders.

"She's not coming, is she?" I said, glancing back at the clock on the front of the town hall. It read 10.20.

"Look how nuts Megan's parents were acting yesterday," said TJ. "They probably left for home last night! Bet Megan's waking up in her own bed right about now, with her ears still ringing from the yelling-at that Naomi got on the way home!"

"Maybe. . ." I shrugged, feeling myself being shoved sideways, with a wave of human movement. "I just thought she might have texted if that happened."

"Hey, look! It's the Gala Princess float! And there's Ellie!" Rachel called out, as a lorry bedecked in giant pastel flowers and lots of smiling, waving girls turned into the high street.

We were expecting to see Ellie. Sandra, the owner of the Style Compony Salon, had seen her win the talent show final and thought she was adorable, and asked her to come on-board the Gala Princess float as a flower girl. Her job was to sit at the foot of the Princess's (cardboard) throne and scatter petals from a basket into the crowd. It was *right* up Ellie's street. She could even wear her fairy wings, feather boa and plastic tiara.

"But why's Ellie sitting *on* the throne?" Rachel

suddenly frowned, as the float braked to a standstill, to let the lorries up ahead carefully manoeuvre round the corner on to the prom.

"Is she?" said TJ, standing on his tiptoes and *still* not seeing over the tall people blocking his view.

"Hold on – there's April at the back of the float. I'll ask her what's going on. . ."

"Who's April again?" I asked TJ, as I watched Rachel walk forward and beckon a pretty blonde girl in her late teens to bend over and talk to her.

"One of Amber from the café's sisters. All three of them are on the float every year, since their mum's salon sponsors the Princess thing."

"Oh, yeah, of course!" I nodded, remembering what Mrs Riley had said the other day, and also spotting another pretty blonde in her late teens, like April (Ashleigh, was it?). And then there was a very miserable-looking Amber perched on the back of the float, half-heartedly waving a plastic tulip and looking like she'd rather be in the Antarctic in a bikini than where she was right now.

"Quick!" Rachel called out, waving me and TJ towards her. "April says we can get on the lorry while it's stopped. Come on – let's get out of the crowd!"

I felt a shudder of nerves, looking at the two

wide metal rungs that Rachel was already climbing up.

"*Yesss!!*" TJ laughed, beating me to it and scrambling up the mini-ladder after Rachel.

"But what about Megan?" I called out.

"She's not going to come now, Stella," said Rachel. "Get up here quick – before the lorry starts up again!"

And so I got up there, my elbows grabbed and hoisted by Rachel and TJ.

"Right, grab some of this and chuck, chuck!" ordered Rachel, handing us a fistful of confetti each and pointing to the crowd.

"Hey, Rach," said TJ, doing what he was told and flinging with one hand, while waving at his deliriously grinning sister perched up on the throne with the other. "Did you find out from April how come Ellie's sitting in the Gala Princess's seat?"

"Yeah I did. April said the organizers still hoped 'Svetlana' would show this morning, even though she didn't turn up for her crowning yesterday," Rachel explained hurriedly, as she expertly threw arcs of confetti into the crowd (hey, that's what comes of years of practice, I guess). "They did ask the runner-up to come along today, just in case. But her mother phoned at the last minute to say her daughter didn't want to be thought of as second-best and wouldn't be coming."

"So they opted for Ellie instead?" I said, starting to feel less self-conscious about being up here as I watched the crowds laughing and reaching to grab the flurries of confetti I was throwing.

"Yeah," Rachel replied, "'cause – oh, hey, isn't that your mobile, Stella?"

That was funny – I hadn't heard the ringtone. Quickly, I pulled it out of my pocket to check.

"Er . . . it's not ringing, Rach. You must be hearing things!"

Rachel stopped her confetti-chucking and frowned at the phone – at the *exact* same time as it warbled into life.

"Uh . . . hello?" I mumbled warily, as me and Rachel both stared in surprise at each other.

"STELLA!" a voice shouted in my ear. "STELLA, it's ME! Can you see me? Here, CATCH!!"

"Megan?! Megan, where are you?" I asked, glancing around in the current crush of the crowd and suddenly spotting a rolled-up newspaper come *hurtling* through the air in my direction.

"Whoah – I've got it!" yelled TJ, expertly catching the paper as it sailed past my head.

"I'm here! I'm over HERE!! See?" Megan's voice

shouted into the phone pressed to my ear.

"*There* she is!" said Rachel, pointing our friend out.

And there she was, pogo-ing on the spot outside the fish 'n' chip shop, her arm arcing above her head in an enthusiastic wave.

Standing right behind her was Mrs Sticky Toffee, giving me a wiggle-of-the-fingers wave with what looked like a stick of Portbay rock.

"Look – Megan came!" I said, turning quick to make sure TJ had clocked her too.

He had – like me and Rachel, he'd stopped his confetti-chucking duties and was waving back at her just as frantically.

"What happened, Megan? We waited for you this morning!" I turned back and asked into the mobile.

(Er . . . that was weird: Mrs S-T – and her stick of rock – had just disappeared.)

"The traffic . . . was TERRIBLE! Mum and Dad are parked *streets* away," Megan panted breathlessly as she pogoed herself into view and out again. "I can't stay . . . 'cause we're . . . on our way home!!"

"How's everything?" I shouted into the mobile, so she could hear me above the din of the crowd.

"Did your parents go mad at you yesterday?"

"NO!" I spotted Megan grin. "They're not mad at ME any more! Bit mad at Naomi, though! Look . . . I've got to go . . . check out the newspaper. . .!"

"I will!" I told her, glancing round and seeing that TJ was already flicking through it, confetti stuck in his hair and eyelashes.

"And E-MAIL me!" I heard her voice say, though the lorry had already started rumbling around the corner and Megan had slipped out of sight. "Send me an attachment with those photos from our Gala Muppet night, if you ca—"

"Megan? Can you hear me? I can't see you any more," I babbled, frantically scanning the crowds. "If you can hear me, BYE!!"

"Does she have to go? Quick, let me say bye properly too!" Rachel urged, stopping her waving efforts and reaching for my mobile.

"Signal's gone," I told her, and was surprised to see how misty with disappointment her brown eyes suddenly became.

To everyone staring up at the Gala Princess float, me, TJ and Rachel must have looked like we'd clambered on the wrong lorry; from the dejected looks on our faces, we'd have probably suited the local undertaker's float better (if there'd been such a depressing thing).

"Let's take a look at the paper, then!" said TJ, all of a sudden remembering what he was holding in his hand. "Where's the article about us. . .? Hey, get this! It's practically a whole page!"

And it was. A huge picture of me (holding up the locket), Megan (holding up the metal detector), Ellie (cuddling super digging-machine Bob), with Rachel and TJ too, of course. And not forgetting the star of the shot – Joseph's house.

"'*Teen Sleuths Uncover Long-lost Local Secret*'," Rachel read out, struggling to keep her balance as the float stopped, started, and juddered towards the prom.

"Looks like it says everything you told them, Stella!" TJ said excitedly, his head down, skim-reading the feature. "And listen to this bit. . . The paper want to start a campaign to raise money to save the chandelier before the house is demolished! And they've got the organizers of the Gala to start them off with a big donation!"

"You're kidding!" I gasped, my heart skipping a beat or three.

"Wait a minute . . . there's more," TJ continued, flipping the paper over so we could see the facing page. "Check *this* out. . . They've printed a photo of that painting in the museum – the one they think is Joseph all grown up. It says here that they're running an appeal to see if anyone can solve the mystery of what happened to him!"

Wow. . .

My head was so full of wow that I overbalanced and lurched into a giant daffodil as the lorry finally braked to a halt. But I could have lurched into a field of thistles and nettles and I wouldn't have cared less.

'Cause I'd just realized that little old me – shy-girl Stella Stansfield – had made a difference to the world.

OK, to just a small, sandy, seasidey corner of the world, but that was still pretty wow to me.

And as I waved across at my surprised-to-see-me Mum, Dad and twin brothers, I knew that – wow – there was nowhere else I'd rather be than this sandy, seasidey corner of the world.

But *wow*, I wished the Portbay Youth Orchestra hadn't started parping and squeetling just now and ruined a beautiful moment. . .

From: Frankie
To: *stella*
Subject: Don't you 4get about me!

Hi Stella!

You sound like you've been having *way* too much fun lately. Now that wouldn't be a problem, except for the fact that YOU'RE HAVING *WAY* TOO MUCH FUN, WITHOUT *ME*!

Only kidding (ish). I mean, it's brilliant that you've got all these new mates, honest it is. But if I thought for a *second* that you're forgetting about me and your old friends back in Kentish Town, we'd all be straight down to Portbay on the train to sort you out! Actually, all coming down on the train to Portbay sounds excellent!! Can you imagine us all sitting in that dumb, old-fashioned café, ordering sundaes from that grumpy waitress that spilt the spaghetti over your head when I visited you?

Wonder if I could get the girls organized to do it, or is it getting too near the end of the holidays? (Sorry – I mentioned the end of the holidays. That's a bit like swearing, isn't it?)

In the meantime, I order you to text me every

half-hour for the next four hours as punishment for having all that fun without me. I expect the first one in approximately ten seconds' time . . . ha!

Miss you ☹, but M8s 4eva ☺!

Frankie xxx

STOP PRESS!! Hey, an e-mail from you JUST jumped on to my screen. What's all this about you doing a makeover on the grumpy girl who works at the café? Hope you made her look awful, to get back at her for splatting that spaghetti on your head! Write back instantly (if not sooner) and tell me *everything*. . .

Want to know more. . .?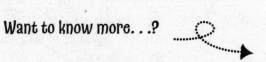

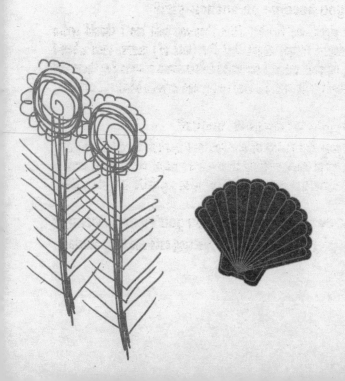

Meet the sparkly-gorgeous Karen McCombie!

★ **Describe yourself in five words. . .**

Scottish, confident, shy, calm, ditzy.

★ **How did you become an author-girl?**

When I was eight, my teacher Miss Thomson told me I should write a book one day. I forgot about that for (lots of) years, then when I was working on teen mags, I scribbled a few short stories for them and suddenly thought, "Hmmm, I'd love to try and write a book . . . can I?"

★ **Where do you write your books?**

In the loft room at the top of our house. I work v. hard 'cause I only have a little bit of book-writing time – the rest of the day I'm making Playdough dinosaurs or pretend "cafés" with my little daughter, Milly.

★ **What else do you get up to when you're not writing?**

Reading, watching DVDs, eating crisps, patting cats and belly dancing!

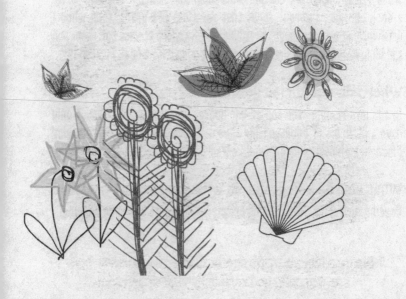